Journey – to the – End of the Earth

Dave & Neta Jackson

Illustrated by Anne Gavitt

BETHANY HOUSE PUBLISHERS
MINNEAPOLIS, MINNESOTA 55438

Story illustrations by Anne Gavitt.
Cover design and illustration by Catherine Reishus McLaughlin.

Scripture quotations are from the King James Version of the Bible.

Published by Bethany House Publishers
A Ministry of Bethany Fellowship International
11400 Hampshire Avenue South
Minneapolis, Minnesota 55438
www.bethanyhouse.com

Printed in the United States of America by
Bethany Press International, Minneapolis, Minnesota 55438

Library of Congress Cataloging-in-Publication Data

Jackson, Dave.
Journey to the end of the earth : William Seymour / by Dave & Neta Jackson ; illustrations by Anne Gavitt.
p. cm. — (Trailblazer books)
Summary: In 1906, while visiting his journalist uncle in California, thirteen-year-old Jerry hears the San Francisco earthquake predicted at preacher William Seymour's Pentecostal mission, sees the ensuing destruction, and learns the power of the Holy Ghost.
ISBN 0–7642–2266–X (pbk.)
1. Earthquakes—California—San Francisco—Juvenile fiction. [1. Earthquakes—California—San Franciso—Juvenile fiction. 2. Seymour, William Joseph, 1870–1922—Fiction. 3. San Francisco (Calif.)—Fiction. 4. Journalism—Fiction. 5. Afro-Americans—Fiction. 6. Uncles—Fiction. 7. Christian life—Fiction.] I. Jackson, Neta. II. Gavitt, Anne, ill. III. Title.
PZ7.J132418 Jo 2000
[Fic] dc21 00–010470

Other than being dramatized, all events depicting William Seymour and the Azusa Street Mission are true. Eleven-year-old Lawrence Catley, who was healed of TB, grew up to serve as a soldier in World War I and to live a long and productive life thereafter. However, it was not our fictional Jerry Newman but a neighbor lady who urged Lawrence to attend the Azusa Street Mission.

The Newmans and Romburg, Texas, are entirely fictional with one notable exception. On April 17, 1906, the night before the great San Francisco earthquake, a reporter from the *Los Angeles Daily Times* did visit the Azusa Street Mission and wrote up his opinions as quoted herein, including the prophesy of destruction. That article was published the same day the headlines announced the earthquake.

In the days immediately after the earthquake, Frank Bartleman distributed his tract "The Last Call" in trains and depots around Los Angeles. But he also wrote a special "Earthquake Tract" that came off the press on Tuesday, April 24.

It should also be noted that the first issue of William Seymour's newspaper, *The Apostolic Fire,* did not actually come out until September 1906, six months after the date we used for the sake of this story.

CONTENTS

DAVE AND NETA JACKSON are a full-time husband/wife writing team who have authored and coauthored many books on marriage and family, the church, relationships, and other subjects. Their books for children include the TRAILBLAZER series and *Hero Tales,* volumes I, II, and III. The Jacksons have two married children, Julian and Rachel, and make their home in Evanston, Illinois.

Chapter 1

Holy Ghost Fire

FOR AS LONG AS I CAN REMEMBER, my mama used to say, *"Gerald Fredrick Newman, if'n you don't straighten up, I'm gonna ship you off to the end of the earth."* Well, I guess she's finally gone and done it. She put me on the train this very morning—April 3, 1906, a real red-letter day as far as I'm concerned. I'm on my way to Los Angeles, California, right on the edge of the Pacific Ocean—nearly the end of the earth to her. But if you ask me . . . well, I never let on what I *really* thought of going to California to stay with my uncle Thomas.

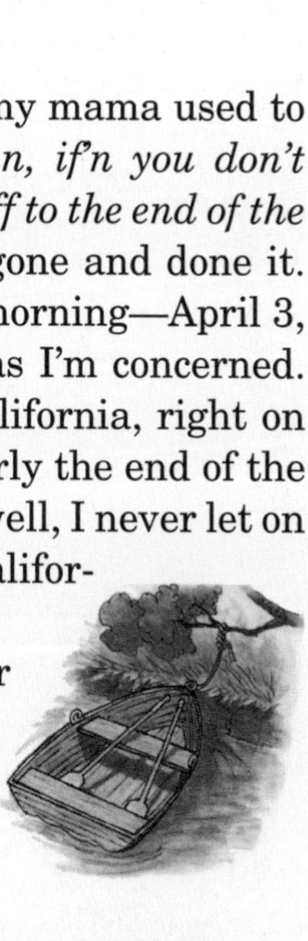

Instead, I played a little Brer Rabbit, saying, "Please don't send me to the end of the earth, Mama," when that was exactly where I wanted to go, especially since my uncle Thomas is the first Negro reporter with the *Los Angeles Daily Times*. He's always writing stories about bank robbers and horse races and ships lost at sea. He sends us clippings from time to time, and that's what made me decide that I want to be a reporter, too. That's why the brier patch I'm headed for is just where I want to be. And I'm getting out of school, to boot!

I can't really blame Mama for sending me away, though. It seems like the taller I've grown this past year, the more trouble I've gotten in. It's like hitting my head on things I don't know are there. But maybe that's just what happens when you turn fourteen and can't seem to find all your arms and legs half the time.

Take that day a couple weeks ago when Rodney Costner said, "Hey, Jerry, let's cut school to go fishin'." Well, Mr. Michael had never complained before when we borrowed his old rowboat without asking. He kept it tied up just north of town where Menard's Bayou dumps into Trinity River. Menard's Bayou is a meandering channel of slow-moving water that sometimes opens into small lakes, draining the woods all the way up into Polk County. Fishin's good there because there's no other way into that swampy wilderness. Anyway, we jumped in that little boat and rowed quietly like two ghosts floating above a morning fog that rose a couple feet above the dark water. Once we got to where we thought no one could see us, we let her drift and set to fishin'. It didn't take long until Rod hooked a big ol' bass. I mean, he was a real lunker!

"Keep him out of the weeds," I said, shielding my eyes to see down into that dark water from which a mist still rose. I hoped that bass would give us a jump or two.

By then Rod was standing up, horsing that fish in with his bamboo pole bent nearly double. I stood up, too, and reached out to get ahold of the string. He didn't have any real fishing line, and I was sure that huge largemouth would break his line. Rod and I were yellin' and shoutin' advice back and forth, when suddenly there was a sickening crunch, and my left foot went right through the bottom of that old boat and into cold water that seemed as thick as Texas oil.

Losing my balance, I lunged forward to catch ahold of the gunwale and nearly tipped us over. It knocked Rod off his feet, and he fell backward into the bottom of the boat, losing hold of his pole, which disappeared without a trace into the bayou after that escaping bass.

As water gushed in, I struggled to pull my foot back up through the hole. But my shoe caught on the jagged edge of the boards, and I was stuck. I pulled and I yanked. The thought of me trapped in that boat as it sunk to the bottom of Menard's Bayou gave me the strength of a bull, and I jerked my foot free . . . only my shoe didn't come with it and the water gushed in all the faster.

Even though Rod is as good a swimmer as I am, he turned his wild eyes toward me. "Come on, Jerry.

Let's get to shore," he said and rolled over the edge of the boat.

"Wait!" I said, but he had already disappeared under the water.

By the time he came up for air ten feet away, I had one hand on each side of the boat, which was quickly sinking out from under me. "Rod, wait. I gotta find my shoe. It came off."

"What am I supposed to do about it? Just put your shoe back on and swim to shore."

"I can't—my shoe's not in the boat. It came off under the boat when I pulled my foot back through. Mark the spot and help me dive for it!"

He bobbed under and came up sputtering, "I ain't divin' for your old shoe. This water's cold, and there's water moccasins in here!"

As he splashed toward the densely forested bank, what was left of the rowboat drifted slowly away from the place where I'd lost my shoe, so I dove in and went after the shoe myself. Down I went once—Rod was right; it was cold—and a second time. Usually I can grab a handful of mud under ten feet of water, but somehow all the excitement and Rod's talk of water moccasins left me breathless and panicky. I couldn't seem to stay down for more than a few seconds. Under I went again and again until I finally spotted my old shoe caught in a bunch of weeds not more than three feet from me. Boy, was I glad it hadn't drifted to the bottom and buried itself in muck.

When I surfaced, Rod was already pulling himself out of the water with the help of a moss-covered oak limb that hung out over the water. He sat down on the bank and wiped the water out of his eyes with his arm. "Hurry up, Jerry!" he called. "We gotta get out of here before someone comes."

I looked around and saw Mr. Michael's rowboat slowly floating down the bayou with only a couple inches of freeboard showing above the water. Can you believe it? It was waterlogged as well as rotten.

By the time we had hiked through the woods and returned to town, our clothes were fairly dry. With a little luck, no one would learn about our disastrous fishing trip. But with only 386 people in it (Millie Perkins hadn't had her baby yet), Romburg, Texas, is so small that not much stays a secret for long. By suppertime Mr. Michael was banging on the door of my house. How he found out, I'll never know, but there he was, yelling at Mama while I hid in the other room with my little brothers and sister, hoping he wouldn't come in after me.

"Those boys done stole my fishin' boat and sank it in Trinity River. And I want a cash money payment right now, or I'm goin' to Sheriff Robinson, and they'll be locked up before dark!"

Well, seein' as how it was already almost dark, and Mr. Michael was white—though not much more than white trash, if you ask me—Mama couldn't do much else but dig down into the bottom of her sewing basket, where she kept her savings, and hand him a five-dollar bill. With a look of surprise, he stuffed it in his pocket and stomped off our rickety front porch without another word. But I doubt he got the same from Rod's house. Mr. Costner's a big man, and he'd make mincemeat of Mr. Michael before he'd give him five dollars—Klan or no Klan.

We've had a good deal of trouble between the blacks and whites in these parts lately. The Ku Klux Klan's been getting bolder and bolder, trying to make us pay for the South losing the war, I guess. There was a lynching up near Livingston last fall, and I think Mr. Michael might be a Klan member, but Mama says that if he were a member, he wouldn't bother to wear a hood. It's the "respectable" whites who wear the hood so people won't see who they are.

But five dollars is five dollars, and I really felt bad that Mama had to spend her hard-earned savings to get me out of trouble. Mama says that with four kids to feed, she doesn't have time for me to be a troublemaker. But somehow ever since Papa died last year, trouble seems to follow me around like a puppy after a little boy with corn bread—crumbs being bound to fall. "Boy, you need a man to be raisin' you," Mama will say. But then both of us get tears in our eyes remembering Papa, and we don't say any more. If there's anything I hate worse than cryin', it's seeing Mama cry.

"You gotta quit 'sociatin' with that Costner boy" was the first thing Mama said when the five of us finally sat down to dinner. "Him and all those other shiftless no-goods. Your grades been going down at school, and you forget your chores around the house. If'n you don't straighten up, I'm gonna ship you off to the end of the earth."

I wanted to tell her that it wasn't Rod's fault this time. If I hadn't put my foot through the bottom of Mr. Michael's boat, we'd have had it back safe and sound without him ever knowing. On the other hand, we had kind of stolen it, and we for sure ruined it, not to mention skipping school. So I just kept quiet until my sister got us off the subject by pestering Mama for some more gravy and biscuits.

I worked real hard to be good the next few days, trying every way I knew to avoid trouble. But somehow it wasn't to last.

I used to go to church when I was little, but Papa never went; so as soon as I was old enough, I quit going, too. Mama had been a regular attender, but when Papa died, I think she blamed God, and she never went back to church. The only time she talked about religion was when she was trying to scare us kids into being good with the threat of hellfire. But we didn't pay much attention.

As far as I know, Rodney's family has never gone to church. In fact, Clarence and JoJo, my other two buddies, don't go to church, neither. None of us guys do.

But last Friday night the four of us were over at Rod's house playin' mumblety-peg when JoJo said, "Hey, you all, it's getting too dark for this. We's gonna cut off one of our toes if we keep throwing this knife." Then he looked down the street as if he were hearing a bird calling him. "I know what. They be havin' a revival at the church. Let's go see what's happenin'."

No one needed to ask which church. There are only two churches in Romburg—the Baptist Church, a nice brick building up on the hill for all the white people, and the African Methodist Episcopal Church, a little frame building with peeling paint in a grove of pine trees down by the river.

JoJo was thirteen, same age as me, and always trying to be our leader, so I asked, "Why would we want to go to some revival meeting? You gettin' religion or something?"

"Naw." JoJo threw a rock and hit a fence post square on. "It's just that at revivals, people get happy and start jumping around and singin' and shoutin'. We could watch 'em through the windows and stuff."

"But they'd see us, and then we'd get in trouble," said Rod.

JoJo hesitated, so I said, "No, they wouldn't. It's gettin' too dark. Let's go."

So we sneaked on down there, and sure enough, they were singing and clapping and carrying on like the Lord Almighty was about to visit them. The church was built up on posts about two feet off the ground to protect it from flooding when the Trinity River overflowed its banks, which seemed to happen about every other spring. That left an open crawl space underneath the whole building. Out from under the edges of the building grew grass, stretching tall for the light. But, of course, at this time of the

year, it was dry and yellow.

The windows were high enough for us to walk right up under them without anyone seeing us. Nevertheless, we bent double as we scampered across the open ground to the side of the church. I ducked down behind a dried-out old Christmas tree that was lying in the tall grass next to the building as though it could hide me. A few strands of tinsel decorations still hung from its brittle branches, shimmering like icicles in the last light of the evening.

Even though the late-March evenings were still cool, the windows stood open a few inches to let in fresh air, and we could clearly hear everything that was going on.

Rev. Mason's deep voice boomed, "Glory, glory, glory! Won't that be some fine day when the Lord comes back for His saints? Can I have a witness?"

And the congregation echoed, "Amen!" "That's right!" "Now you're preachin'."

"Our text," continued Rev. Mason, "comes from Acts, chapter two, verses one through four. Listen now as Sister Gentry reads us from the Book."

There was a moment of shuffling, and then a thin voice whined,

> "And when the day of Pentecost was fully come, they were all with one accord in one place. And suddenly there came a sound from heaven as of a rushing mighty wind, and it filled all the house where they were sitting. And there appeared unto them cloven tongues like as of fire, and it sat upon each of them. And they were all filled with the Holy Ghost, and began to speak with other tongues, as the Spirit gave them utterance."

"Thank you, sister. May the Lord add a blessing to the reading of His Word!" said Rev. Mason, and the congregation chorused, "Amen."

Then he continued. "Now, wouldn't that be glorious if right here in Romburg A.M.E. Church on this very night the Holy Ghost was to visit us and fill us with His power so that . . ."

While Rev. Mason continued, my mind drifted to a vision of little flames dancing all around that first church and then coming in through the windows and doors and floating around like butterflies until each flame landed on someone's head. What a sight.

Suddenly I had an idea. I hit the other guys on their shoulders and beckoned with my hand to lead them away from the church. JoJo didn't want to come, but once the others followed me, he came along, too. When we were out of earshot and concealed behind some pine trees, I said, "Any of you ever seen any tongues of fire like that?"

In the twilight, I could barely see JoJo screw up his face. "Like what?" he growled.

"Like in the Bible," I said. "You've heard of Holy Ghost fire, haven't you?"

"Yeah, little flames sat on everyone's head, like each one was a big candle or something," Rod added. Somewhere along the line he'd picked up the story, even though he didn't go to church.

Everyone laughed and then looked at me as if to say, "So?"

I waited a moment to increase the drama. "What if we brought them some Holy Ghost fire tonight?"

Clarence was the first to speak. "What do you mean?"

"Well, back up the road a little way, there's a drainage ditch that has some old cattails in it. What if we picked a few of them cattails, dipped them in some stove oil, and then lit 'em. They'd make perfect torches, 'tongues of fire' that we could wave outside the church windows, and they'd for sure think the Holy Ghost was comin' with fire!"

"Yeah," said JoJo, "and then you'd really see some people gettin' happy. It'd be a show!"

Well, it didn't take us long to pick those cattails and find a bucket of old oil out behind Potter's store. We were back to the woods just about the time Rev. Mason was good and warmed up in his sermon.

The church building had three windows on each side but none in the back, so we went around back to light our torches. The oily cattails made perfect torches, with the flames six inches tall and tapered like large candle flames.

"Keep your torches low until you get in position under a window, then lift them just high enough to be seen," I ordered. Then we divided up—two and two—to march down each side of the church. Rod followed me, and Clarence went with JoJo. When I got to the first window, I whispered back to Rod, "Wait here until I get to the second window. Then we'll hold up the flames at the same time."

He nodded, and I ducked down, holding the torch low so its light wouldn't be seen inside the dimly lit church, and ran around the old Christmas tree to my position under the next window.

Chapter 2

Up in Smoke

I HAD NO SOONER ARRIVED under the second window than I heard a woman's voice begin rising in both volume and pitch as though she were an opera singer warming up for a concert. At the top of the scale she sang one word: "Hallelujah," holding the last syllable long and loud enough to shatter crystal.

And then a man with a booming bass voice began chanting, "Here come the Holy Ghost! Here come the Holy Ghost!"

I lifted my torch above the windowsill and looked to see what Rod was doing. He was doing the same, but we were both laughing so hard that we could hardly stand up.

Then I heard Rev. Mason call out,

"I do believe we have received Holy Ghost fire from on high. Glory! Glory! Glory!"

Rod and I began marching back and forth under our windows, dancing our flaming cattails up and down like the drum major's baton in the Houston Fourth of July parade. Soon the whole church was singing and praising God like a band of angels. Some were shouting praises; some were singing a piece of one song, and some were singing another. I guess they were just too excited to get it all together.

But then I heard the voice of a little girl calling out over all that singing and shouting, "That ain't no Holy Ghost fire! Them's just torches. Look, someone carry 'em on sticks."

Uh-oh! I looked back at Rod. He had stopped marching back and forth and was staring at me as though he were ready to bust from holding his breath.

Rev. Mason said, "Don't you blaspheme the Holy Ghost, child. Those flames are straight from . . . Wait a moment. You right. There *are* sticks under those flames. O Lord, what have we here?"

The congregation's praises and hallelujahs hushed like water when you stopped pumping the handle, and a strange stillness filled the whole pine grove. I didn't know whether to run or dive under the church. Then someone shouted, "It's the Klan. They be comin' to burn us out. Lord a-mercy; it's gotta be the Klan!"

The noise took right up again, except this time it wasn't singing and shouting. It was screams and yells and thuds as benches tipped over and people fell to the floor in their scramble to escape.

"Now, hold on. Hold on, everybody!" called Rev. Mason above the din. "Let's be orderly. It won't do no good to panic. Let's march out of here like the children of Israel. We ain't got nothin' to fear! We ain't been doing nothin' wrong!" But his advice did little good.

Out of the corner of my eye, I saw Rod run for the back of the church—a smart direction to head, I thought, with the church members tumbling out of the front door. Rob had shaken the flame out on his cattail, but a glowing ember on the tip trailed jagged blue smoke as he ran.

I started to follow but twisted my ankle on a bottle or something hidden in the tall grass. I stumbled and fell flat on my face into the prickly Christmas tree. Stabbing pain shot up my leg as I crawled on all fours, struggling to regain my feet. As fast as I could move, I hobbled around to the back of the church and was embraced by the other boys.

"Where's your torch?" asked JoJo.

I shrugged, holding out empty hands. "Let's just get out of here!"

We scampered toward the woods with me holding on to Rod's shoulder like a caboose on a train.

When we gained the cover of the trees, we circled around to get a glimpse of the church. I guess we thought it would be a kick to see the people come down the steps fearing the Klan would be waiting for them. But what we saw when we parted the brush was a fire blazing up the side of the church where the old Christmas tree had been. Thinking it had been set by the Klan, the people were running for their lives. Only Rev. Mason dared turn back to fight the fire. He took off his jacket and began beating at the flames, but in a matter of moments it was out of control.

Finally he stepped back, exhausted, and dropped his coat on the ground. Then with his feet planted wide and his hands on his hips, he looked around, searching the trees at the edge of the clearing. The light from the blaze must have reflected off our faces, because when he saw us, he stopped. He knew we weren't the Klan!

"Hey, you! What you all doing over there? Come here an' give me a hand!"

But by then we were hightailing it out of the area and back toward town.

Without a word, we split up and headed to our homes. In moments I encountered people running the other direction with buckets, headed toward the old church. Even some white people joined in the fire brigade. I wanted to go back, too, and see if I could help or at least see if the church actually burned down, but I was afraid of getting caught. It was obvious to me what had happened—when I fell, my torch had dropped into that dry Christmas tree, and it had gone up in a flash. Somehow I felt like "Fire Starter" was written across my forehead like a Coca-Cola sign. So I kept slinking along toward home, hoping no one would notice me.

When no one was around, I looked back over my

shoulder and studied the dark sky. "O Lord, don't let this be so," I said under my breath. But there it was, an orange glow reflected from a column of smoke rising above the trees. The church was still burning. But maybe . . . maybe with all that help, they would put it out.

I tried to think of a good story to tell Mama if she quizzed me about where I'd been, but all I could think of was whether the guys would tell on me. I hoped not, but then, if someone suspected one of them, all bets were off. Why should one of them take the blame, when I had started the fire?

I took comfort in telling myself that I had been at the wrong place at the wrong time, as though the whole incident had been a tragic accident. But I knew it wasn't. Oh, I hadn't intended to fall into that Christmas tree and light the fire, but it was no accident that we were outside the church with torches in our hands. And that part had been *my* idea! If I was in the wrong place at the wrong time, it was because I shouldn't have been there at all. I just shouldn't have been there!

When I got home, I went around back and gathered an armload of wood and brought it in the house, hoping Mama would think I'd been around the house the whole time, but she hardly even noticed me. My brothers and sister were pestering her something fierce about going to watch the fire, but she was determined to keep them in the house.

"For the last time, the answer is NO. Now, sit down at the table. It's time to eat, and I am dead tired from doing laundry all day."

We all sat down and Mama prayed.

"Why didn't you pray for the people's house that burned?" my sister asked.

"Gloria, I don't want to hear another word about that FIRE!" declared Mama. And when she spoke in that tone of voice, anyone who disobeyed was a fool, so nothing more was said.

I was starting to feel some relief, like maybe I was going to get by without getting in trouble—heaven knows I didn't intend to start that fire. But when I went to bed, I began to think about what Rev. Mason had said to the little girl who spotted our "sticks," as she called them. *"Don't you blaspheme the Holy Ghost, child."*

What did that mean? Were we blaspheming the Holy Ghost by making fun with those flames? What did blaspheming mean, anyway? I tossed and turned in bed, but I couldn't get the questions out of my mind.

"Please, God, let this day be a bad dream. Make that church still be standing, and I'll never blaspheme again."

But the next day when I casually walked down that way to see if God had answered my prayer, I could smell the burned-out church long before I could see the charred timbers standing there like a toppled flower trellis.

It was Sunday morning, April 1—April Fools day—and I was trying to come up with a really good trick to play on my brothers and sister, when Mama called me in from the backyard. "Jerry, sit down."

Whenever she spoke to me that way, I knew something was wrong.

"Jerry, I've heard some talk that connects you and your friends to that fire at the church the other night." She waited and watched as I tried to avoid looking her in the eye. "You know anything 'bout that?"

I swallowed hard. "Yes, ma'am."

She sighed long and deep as she leaned back in her chair and crossed her arms and just sat there shaking her head.

After several moments I said desperately, "It was an accident, Mama! I never meant to start that fire."

"I should hope not. If I thought you did it deliberate, I'd march you down to Sheriff Robinson myself."

We continued to sit silently in the warm kitchen with me not looking at Mama until I heard her sniff a couple times and knew she was crying again. "Come on, Mama. Please don't cry."

"Don't be tellin' me not to cry, young man, after you cause me so much grief. I'll cry if I want to. Yes, sir, I'll cry if I want—until you straighten up."

She was quiet for a few more moments and then said, "Besides, what I'm crying about is missin' your papa. I just can't raise you proper without a man."

I expected her to say, "If'n you don't straighten up, I'm gonna ship you off to the end of the earth," but instead she murmured, "Maybe I could send you to stay with your uncle Thomas. He's your papa's brother and could give you a firm hand."

Uncle Thomas . . . in Los Angeles? I could hardly get my mind around the idea. California *was* practically the end of the earth, right on the edge of the Pacific Ocean. But if Mama thought I was excited to go to California, she might not let me go. So I whined, "How could you do that? It's so far away."

"Don't think I won't do it!" she warned. "There are trains between here an' there, and I'll just put you on one of them and send you out there."

"But that would cost a lot of money. You can't afford—"

"Don't you be tellin' me what I can and can't do. You hear me? If I don't use that sewing basket money to get you straightened out, I'll end up havin' to spend it on payin' for your foolishness, and you still won't be straightened out."

"But, but—" I could see that the more objections I offered, Mama was getting more and more determined to send me to California, but I didn't want to push it too far. So I just said, "Oh, nothin'."

"No. You were gonna say somethin'. You had some other objection to me doin' what I gotta do, so out with it!"

"Well . . . how you know Uncle Thomas is even there? He might be off reportin' on . . . on one of them flying machines, or a revolution somewhere."

She sat there looking at the back door for a long time as though if she stared hard enough she could see right through it and all the way to California. "Nope!" she announced and looked me in the eye with a determined squint. "You stay right here. You're not to leave this house for any reason! You understand?"

"Yes, ma'am."

As she got up and marched out of the house, I thought I'd gone too far and killed the whole idea. She was gone for over an hour, and I began to worry that she had given up her plans to reform me and had decided to go to Sheriff Robinson and tell him what I'd done.

When she finally came back, all she said was "I should have been takin' you children to church all along, but now you've fixed it so there ain't any church to go to. What a fine mess."

Later that day, after we'd had our dinner, I decided I'd go check with the other guys and see whether they'd heard any gossip floating around about the fire. I did the dishes without having to be told and then said, "Mama, can I go out for a while?"

"Not a chance!" she snapped back at me—she hadn't cooled off at all. "I told you that you were to stay in this house, and that's where you'll stay unless I send you out for some wood!"

It didn't sound good. It was one thing to be sent "to the end of the earth," but it was quite another to be locked up in the house like it was a jail.

After a few minutes I said, "Mama, probably Uncle Thomas is at home, don't you think? He'd have written us a letter if he was traveling on some exciting assignment."

"Don't you worry 'bout what ain't none o' your business. I'll know soon enough."

The next morning as I sat in a rickety kitchen chair, pulling on my shoes, Mama planted her hands on her hips and scowled at me. "Where you think you're goin'?"

"School." At least there I could talk to my friends.

She shook her head. "Boy, you ain't heard me yet, have you? You're not goin' nowhere till I say!" She folded her large blue polka-dotted bandana into a triangle, flipped it over her head, and tied the two ends together in front on her forehead and tucked the third end in over the top over her head. "I told you that you're stayin' in this house. Only the little ones'll be goin' to school today."

Oh . . . this was getting bad!

As she put a shawl around her shoulders and hustled my brothers and sister out the door, she looked back at me, and I could see tears in her eyes. Her face seemed softer. "Jerry, it would be a big help to me if you cleaned the house while I'm out. I should be back afore too long."

Remembering how sad she looked when she walked out the door, I cleaned like the Queen of Egypt was coming to visit us. It felt like the least I could do. I didn't want to be such a burden on Mama, but what was done was done.

When she returned, she clutched a small yellow sheet of paper in her left hand. Even from across the room, I could read the words *Western Union* at the top. "What'cha got there, Mama?"

"It's a telegraph from your uncle Thomas. I wired him yesterday askin' if he would take you in for a while. You'll be leavin' on the train tomorrow morning."

Chapter 3

Newspaper Man

WELL, THAT'S HOW I ENDED UP headed for California. Mama packed me some hard-boiled eggs, biscuits, and oranges in our old carpetbag along with my clothes and put me on the local train headed down to Houston. That's as far away from home as I'd ever been, having gone there for the Fourth of July with Papa just before he got sick and died.

This time, as I arrived in Houston, I was wearing Papa's tweed porkpie hat and was off on an adventure of my own. At the station, I had to transfer to the big Southern Pacific train heading to California. It was pretty scary for me not knowing whether I'd get on the right car or whether they would accept my ticket. But everything worked out just fine.

I found a seat near the back of a coach car with a little sign over it that said *Colored*. There were other black people there, but most of them seemed to work on the train as porters and cooks. Somewhere near the front of the train there must have been a dining car, probably just for rich white people, though.

I rode with my face to the window, watching the Texas landscape pass by until my tired eyes kept "thinking" everything I looked at was still moving past me, even when I was looking at something that was not moving. It made me feel kind of dizzy. When the afternoon sun had dropped low enough in the sky to give everything a golden tinge, we began to pass more and more houses and small towns, occasionally stopping for a few minutes at some of them. Finally, as the sun kissed the west, a black porter came through the coach announcing, "San Antonio, San Antonio's our next stop. There'll be a thirty-minute layover for dinner in the restaurant."

Mama had packed me a basket of food, so I didn't need to spend any money for food, but I sure needed to use a rest room. We had stopped in a couple other towns for two or three minutes each, but the only rest rooms in the stations said *Whites Only*, and I didn't dare take the time to go searching for a "colored" rest room, even if there was such a thing. The train wouldn't have waited until I returned, but I knew that for a black boy to go into a "white" rest room was just asking to be tarred and feathered or maybe even lynched.

At least with a thirty-minute stop in San Antonio, if I had to walk back down the tracks to get out of town, I'd have time. But even though we were rolling past houses and businesses and warehouses on either side of the track, the train hadn't started to slow. San Antonio was a big city. I'd have to run miles back down the track to get to the country.

I didn't know what to do. Thinking that I was almost to a rest room made waiting all that much harder.

Suddenly we were passing another train—a freight train—that was stopped on a siding track. I heard our engine's whistle blow. We were finally stopping. On the other side of the train, the station came into view. I got up and moved toward the door, intent on being the first one out onto the platform. Maybe I could sneak back across the tracks and find a secluded spot on the other side of the freight train.

When the train stopped, the people behind me pushed me out first, all right, but it was right into the middle of a crowd of people waiting to meet the train. And the flow of the people behind me swept me along with them right into the train station. Before I knew it, I was through the door and facing a black porter who pointed at me and then pointed to his left while the rest of the people were going to his right.

I knew what direction he meant for me to go, but for some reason I continued to move with the crowd until he reached out and grabbed my arm. "Where you think you're going, boy? Coloreds in there." And he gave me a shove into a small side room.

I didn't have time to be upset with him, because as soon as I entered the room, I saw a sign by a door on the far wall for the colored rest room, and I went straight for it.

When I came out, very much "rested," I saw that this small waiting room had several black people in it, possibly passengers from other coaches on my train or maybe people waiting for some other train. But there was also a woman standing in the corner with a large basket of box lunches that she was selling for a nickel apiece. They looked good, but I still had the food Mama had packed for me back on the train.

I walked back out onto the platform. The sun had set, leaving the sky a swirl of oranges and lavenders, churned by the silhouetted steam and smoke rising from the softly sighing engine at the front of our train. As I waited for the other passengers to finish their dinner, I strolled from one end of the platform to the other. This was great!—off on an adventure to the end of the earth.

The train whistle shrieked, and the conductor rallied the passengers back onto the train by calling, "All aboard! All aboard for El Paso, Tucson, and points west!" I hurried back to my coach, then waited patiently while the white folks climbed the steps and found their way to their seats. I barely got on before the train started moving.

Inside, small kerosene lamps had been lit to give a soft, inviting glow to the coach, but when I got to my seat, I didn't feel so welcomed. There was a problem, a big problem. My carpetbag with my clothes and food was missing. I had left it on my seat so people would know someone was sitting there, but it was gone. I looked on the floor under my seat and in the rack above, but it wasn't to be found.

" 'Scuse me," I said to the white conductor as he came through the car collecting the tickets of those who had just boarded. "Someone has taken my carpetbag that I had—"

"Talk to a porter. I don't have anything to do with collecting trash."

"But it wasn't trash," I protested as he walked on past me and through the back door to the next car.

I kept searching until a new passenger who had taken a seat across the aisle and three rows forward turned around and barked, "Are you going to settle down back there, or should I have you thrown off the train?"

I took my seat, feeling hungrier than ever. Someone had stolen my carpetbag with the food that was supposed to last me all the way to California. I looked out the window. We were already out of the city. I cupped my hands against the window to see out into the dark, but the tears in my eyes turned the light from occasional farmhouses into a glittering blur that I tried to blink away.

By then, heading off to the end of the earth seemed a rather foolish and lonely venture as the train raced along, rocking from side to side to its *clickety-clack, clickety-clack* rhythm. If only I hadn't gotten in so much trouble! I could be home right now having one of Mama's hot meals.

A couple hours later when the porter came through to dim the lamps, I didn't even ask him about my carpetbag. I just curled up in my seat, glad that no one was sitting next to me and glad for the darkness that hid my tear-streaked face. I pulled my hat low and before long, fell asleep.

"El Paso. El Paso in fifteen minutes. Hot coffee, tea, and fresh muffins."

I woke up and looked out. The sun was up and the landscape had changed completely. Gone were the lush green fields and thick woods of east Texas. We were chugging through a rough, barren wasteland of rock and sand and sagebrush. I searched for some sign of civilization but saw nothing more than a distant windmill beside a watering tank. One scraggly tree stood nearby. Deep gorges laced the landscape as though a giant bear had clawed away all the good soil. How could anyone live in this wilderness?

And then we crossed what looked like a dry riverbed with nothing but a muddy stream snaking its way back and forth across the bottom. Three longhorned cattle stood by the stream, one drinking from the stream. I'd heard about cattle country. That's how *people* lived out here, but what did the *cattle* eat? There didn't seem to be a blade of grass anywhere.

Suddenly we were passing corrals and fences and an occasional adobe house. Soon there were more, and the train began to slow until we stopped at the El Paso station. Most people got off the train, stretching their arms and yawning as they made their way into the station. The coffee and muffins smelled so good! My stomach growled loudly enough that I looked around to see if anyone noticed.

" 'Scuse me," I said, approaching one of the porters who was carrying luggage for a fancy-dressed Spanish woman getting off the train. "Where's the rest room?" I asked.

He pointed to two doors—one for women and one for men—which I had already seen. "No, *I* need one," I whispered.

"This is El Paso, son. Ain't no separate facilities. Just go on in."

"You mean we have to use the same as whites?"

"That's right. You might wait till most people have come out. But no one from round here will bother you."

He was right. Some of the other black people from the train were going in and out of the rest rooms, so I did, too. And no one complained.

Mama had given me fifteen cents, so I spent a nickel for a cup of hot chocolate and a muffin. I think it was the best muffin I'd ever eaten, even though I'm usually partial to Mama's cookin'.

Two days later the train pulled into the Los Angeles station with its elegant Spanish architecture of red-tiled roofs and thick-walled arches that gave the impression of whitewashed adobe. I was so hungry that when I came down the train steps, I clung to the handrail for fear my shaky knees would collapse.

Once on firm ground, I just stood there looking for my uncle as the other passengers moved by me. I tried to remember how he looked. I knew that with his suits and ties, his waved hair, and his pencil-thin mustache, he was a classier version of my father, but suddenly I couldn't remember what my father looked like. The harder I tried, the more his image escaped me. How could I possibly have forgotten what my own father looked like? I felt like I was going crazy. And how would I ever recognize my uncle Thomas if I couldn't remember what his brother—my father—looked like?

I walked back and forth on the platform and in and out of the station, but all the black men seemed to either be working for the railroad or already connected with family or friends. There was no handsome black man standing around by himself looking for me.

As the train had come into Los Angeles, we had ridden past houses and neighborhoods for half an hour before we arrived at the station. This wasn't like Romburg or Houston, or even San Antonio. It was huge. I couldn't just walk down the street asking where Thomas Newman lived. On the other hand, maybe I could. He was a famous newspaper reporter. Certainly most people would know who he was and where he lived.

Feeling a little less shaky now that I had a plan for finding my uncle, I went back into the train station and walked up to a white boy just about my age standing near the front door that led out to the street. He was holding up a newspaper and shouting, "Extra! Extra! Read all about it! Red Car Line to extend service to Santa Ana by June!"

I approached him and waited for him to finish, but he just kept shouting his "Extra! Extra!" speech, glancing at me once and then ignoring me—probably guessing that I wasn't going to buy one of his papers. But I kept standing there until finally he said, "What you looking at?"

"Nothin'. You know where Thomas Newman lives?"

"Who?" He looked at me like I had challenged his "Extra! Extra!" pitch.

"Thomas Newman. He's my uncle."

He looked away, dismissing me. "Never heard of him—Extra! Extra! . . ."

I stepped in front of him. "Wait a minute. He's a famous reporter with your paper." I pointed at the paper he held. "He probably wrote that story you're talking about right now."

The paper boy screwed up his face in disbelief. "About the Red Car Line? Beats me. I can't read."

I was getting nowhere. "Well, then, where do they write these newspapers? My uncle's probably there right now working on a story for tomorrow's paper."

"The *Los Angeles Daily Times* building? That's simple. It's over on First and Broadway. Can't miss it. Go right out this door, turn right, and the first street is First Street. Turn left, go about eight blocks, and you'll be there."

Shaky as I felt for not having eaten very much in two days, I headed out the door and down the street. Los Angeles was magnificent—wide streets with tracks down the middle on which electric streetcars ran every few minutes, and there were automobiles. I counted five of them as I walked. In Romburg there wasn't even one horseless carriage.

I found the *Los Angeles Daily Times* building as easily as the newspaper boy had said. But before going in, I took off my hat and picked at my hair. I wanted to look my best to meet my uncle, but after sleeping three nights on a train, my hair was nappy, and my clothes were wrinkled—but what else could I do?

Inside, the main room of the newspaper building was full of desks with people typing and answering telephones. I didn't know there were so many telephones in the whole world. Clerks were running back and forth as if in a constant relay race. Everything was happening at once. The newspaper business was just as exciting as I had imagined it.

I didn't see my uncle—or any black people, for that matter. But he probably was in the back in his own special office, him being such an important reporter and all.

Finally I stopped a young woman who came past me. She had short black hair and painted lips that looked like a red tulip. "Can you tell me where to find Thomas Newman?" I asked.

She gazed up at the ceiling as though a list of the important reporters was written there, and then after leaving her mouth hanging open for a moment, she said, "Sorry." She looked back at me and shook her head. "I don't think I know him."

"He's an investigative reporter here. He's my uncle."

This time she frowned. "We don't have any colored reporters as far as I know."

"Oh yeah. He works here. He's sent us some of his articles. Some even have his name on them."

"Well, what's he write about?"

"Uh . . ." I thought for a moment. "The last one was about the Stanley Steamer setting the world speed record, 127.6 miles per hour on the beach." I knew the story almost by heart. "Back on January 6."

The woman put her finger beside her cheek and supported her chin with her thumb and frowned. "I remember, but that happened in Florida. We ran an article about it, but we didn't send a reporter back there."

Well, I *thought* I knew the story by heart, but somehow I had never noticed that the record had been set on a Florida beach. Since my uncle had sent me the article from his paper, I had just assumed the record had been set on a California beach.

"Are you sure your uncle's name was on it?" the woman asked.

"Well, no, I guess not on that one. But he sent the article to me. He must have written it."

"Just a minute. You said his name was Thomas Newman?"

When I nodded, she turned and walked back

through the sea of desks with that hurried pace everyone in the newspaper office seemed to use. Suddenly it struck me: If Uncle Thomas went to Florida to report on the Stanley Steamer, why didn't he stop in Texas to see us? He had to have come right through Houston. Something wasn't quite right.

A few minutes later "Miss Tulip-Lips" returned, shaking her head. When she got up to me, she said, "Well, he doesn't work here, but apparently he's a freelance stringer who has occasionally written articles we've printed." She shrugged.

Something was wrong. I was sure I was at the right newspaper—the *Los Angeles Daily Times*. "Well, can . . . can you tell me where he lives?"

"Sorry." She pursed her bright red lips and shook her head. "Our city editor didn't seem to know. He said Mr. Newman just comes in from time to time looking for a lead or to deliver something he's written. But he doesn't know where he lives."

She turned and went on about her business, and I just stood there, feeling like I was in a quicksand bog, going down fast!

Chapter 4

Texas Boy Down

I HADN'T SEEN THE PACIFIC OCEAN YET, but being alone in such a big city unable to find my uncle sure enough made me feel like I had arrived at the end of the earth. And for the first time, "the end of the earth" didn't seem like a very fun place to be!

I thought about waiting there in the newspaper building until my uncle came in, but if the woman was right, he didn't come into the office very often. It might be days before he came in again.

I could go back to the train depot and wait. Maybe Uncle Thomas was out reporting on a bank robbery or some other important assignment and just couldn't get there on time. Maybe he'd come as soon as he could. But somehow, that seemed like a thin hope.

However, there was one person right here in this office who at least knew who my uncle was. That might be as close as I could come to tracking him down.

When Miss Tulip-Lips came past me again, I stopped her and said, "Could you take me back to that man who knows my uncle?"

"The city editor?"

I nodded. She looked up at the ceiling with her mouth open again, and I couldn't help but look up, too. The moment I did it, I felt stupid and imagined that she'd laugh, "Ha, ha. Made you look, you dirty crook." But she didn't. And a moment later she smiled at me and said, "I suppose I could take you to him. Follow me."

Back through that sea of desks we walked to an office just like I had imagined my uncle in, but instead of my uncle sitting behind a fancy desk, a little bald white man sat there with half-moon glasses perched on the end of his nose.

"Mr. Garrison, this is that boy I mentioned to you who's looking for Mr. Newman."

"What now, boy?" He looked at me over the top of his glasses.

"Well, sir," I said as I spun my hat in my hands like it was a steering wheel on one of those new automobiles, "I came from Texas on the train this morning to stay with my uncle, but he didn't pick me up at the station. And so far, you're the only person I've found who knows him."

"Humph," the editor said, frowning as he shuffled some papers on his desk. "I'd hardly say that I *know* him. He writes for us occasionally. He probably lives over in the colored district, but I couldn't say where."

It was time to leave. I could see that the man wanted to return to his paper work, but he was my only lead. "Do you know anyone else who knows him?"

The editor was shaking his head, but he said, "I guess I've seen him with Jeffrey a few times, but—"

"Who's Jeffrey? Please . . ."

"The janitor. Betty, take him to find Jeffrey. I've got to get back to work."

Miss Tulip-Lips made her eyes and her mouth into little circles and beckoned me with her finger, so I followed her as she took me to some stairs that led down to the basement.

"Jeffrey . . . Jeffrey," she began to call when she got to the bottom of the stairs as though the dark hallway before us was some kind of underground tunnel she didn't want to enter. "Oh, Jeffrey."

From a door at the end of the hall stepped a wiry black man with silver hair and bent shoulders. He stood beneath a single, bare light bulb so that, though his hair shone like a halo, we couldn't see his face.

"Yes, ma'am," he said.

"Jeffrey, could you come here and speak with this boy. He thinks you might know his uncle."

Once he had come through the darkness of the hallway to stand with us in the light from the stairwell, he looked me up and down and said, "I don't know you, son."

"No, sir. But I hope you know my uncle, Thomas Newman. He's a reporter who writes for this here newspaper."

"Thomas? Sure. We go back a long way. You kin?"

"Yes, sir. He's my uncle, and I've come all the way from Texas to stay with him, but he didn't meet me at the train. I'm lookin' for someone who knows where to find him."

"Well, I know where he lives, but that don't mean he's at home. Now, if you go out of the front of this building, you can catch the yellow streetcar on First Street. Take it northwest to Alvarado. He lives about four houses from the corner—142 North Alvarado, I think."

I had one nickel left—just enough for that streetcar!

In twenty minutes I was walking up the street to Uncle Thomas's house. When I found the number—we didn't have house numbers in Romburg—it was a small frame house painted white and partially hidden from the street by a couple orange trees and some huge hibiscus bushes. I was so happy to finally arrive at my uncle's house that, with my hat in my hand, I felt like I was knocking on heaven's gate when I rapped on the paint-chipped door.

But it was not Uncle Thomas who answered the door.

Instead, it was a rather heavyset woman about my mother's age. She wore a white apron over her blue print dress, had a white kerchief tied around her head, and a broom in her hand. With an uplifted eyebrow, she waited for me to say the first words.

"Thomas Newman?"

The shadow of a smirk floated across her face as she looked down at herself as if to say, "Honey, do I look like Thomas Newman?" Instead, she politely said, "No. I'm Mrs. Catley."

"But, Mr. Newman—the newspaper reporter. Does he live here?"

"Yes, but he's workin' today." And she began to close the door.

"Oh yeah. Probably on some big story. I'm his nephew." Then I hurriedly added, "Come from Texas to stay with him."

She pulled her head back and looked me up and down. "Land sakes, son. You do favor him a good deal. So you're his nephew, huh? You weren't s'posed to arrive till tomorrow. That's why I'm here fixin' the place up today." She swung the door wide. "Come right in. How'd you get here a day early?"

I stepped into a small, bright living room and could see beyond it toward the back of the house a kitchen on one side and a bedroom on the other. The living room had a small desk with a green-shaded electric lamp—he had electricity in his house—and a typewriter on it, several bookcases, a couple chairs, and along one wall a couch . . . with a boy on it.

The moment I noticed him, the woman said, "Oh, that's my son, Lawrence. He comes with me sometimes. Your name is. . . ?"

"Jerry . . . Jerry Newman." I was still looking at the boy on the couch. He was just lying there with a thin blanket over him, looking at me like I was the one doing a strange thing in the middle of the afternoon.

"Well, isn't this fine," she said, wiping her hands on her apron. "Jerry and Larry. Only I don't call him Larry no more like I used to when he was little." She stopped for a moment, seeing me still watching her son. "Lawrence stays down most of the time 'cause he has TB—tuberculosis. Mr. Newman—your uncle—doesn't mind me bringing him over when I clean. Lawrence likes to read, and your uncle sure has a lot of books."

"TB . . ." I'd heard of that sickness before. I tore my eyes away from the boy on the couch so as not to be staring at him and looked at the shelves with all my uncle's books. "Yeah, lots of books," I said.

"Say, where's your luggage, boy?" Mrs. Catley looked outside as though I had left it there. "Ain't you toting anything?"

"I lost it on the train—stolen, I guess."

"You mean to say, all you've got is the clothes on your back and that sorry hat of yours?"

I looked down at my hat. I didn't think it was such a bad hat. After all, it had been Papa's hat. But she was right. "No, ma'am. I mean, yes, ma'am. This is all I got. In fact, I ain't had nothin' to eat for over two days 'cause all my food was in that carpetbag."

"Good gracious," said Mrs. Catley as she slammed the door and headed into the kitchen. "You wait right there with Lawrence while I fix you somethin' to eat."

A moment later pans banged and cupboards slammed. "You know," she called back from the kitchen, "you and Lawrence are nearly neighbors. We's from Texas, too—from San Antonio."

I sat in a chair, looking at the books on Uncle Thomas's shelves but sneaking glances at Lawrence.

He spoke first. "It was the doctor who said we should come out to California."

I looked at him. "Yeah, I suppose it's pretty nice here."

"It's warm but not so humid as San Antonio." He sat up on the couch, but even that little exertion caused him to cough.

I tried not to pay any attention. "Our train went through San Antonio. Did you come out on the train?"

"Yeah. Our whole family came out." He was silent for a few moments, and then he said, "My father works with your uncle. That's how they met—how Mama came to clean house for your uncle from time to time."

I looked at Lawrence with new admiration. "So what's your father do at the newspaper?"

"Oh, he don't work for the newspaper. He works at the racetrack, mucking out the horse barns." He grinned. "He got me in to see a race once. If I get better again, maybe you can come with us."

But at that moment, I didn't care about any horse race. I was thinking about where he said his father and my uncle worked. Could that be true—that he cleaned out horse barns? It would answer a lot of questions, like why they didn't know him very well at the newspaper. No, it couldn't be true. Uncle Thomas was a famous reporter for a big-city newspaper, the *Los Angeles Daily Times*. If he was working at a racetrack, it must be because he was on assignment doing an undercover investigation. Yeah, that had to be it. He must be fixin' to expose some gambling scandal.

Soon Mrs. Catley brought Lawrence and me steaming bowls of chili and hunks of cold corn bread. "This chili was all I could find in your uncle's refrigerator. I hope it's all right."

It was hot and spicy and probably the best chili I had ever eaten. At least I was hungry enough to think that. My bowl was empty before Lawrence had eaten a third of his. But, then, every few minutes he had to stop eating, coughing so badly I thought he was going to cough up his guts. Suddenly I remembered what tuberculosis was. We called it consumption in Romburg. Most times people died of it after coughing so badly that they coughed up blood. I didn't see any blood, but the towel Lawrence held to his mouth was too dark to notice. His coughing did make tears stream from his eyes, though.

When he stopped and had returned to eating his chili, I asked, "Is California helping you get better like the doctor said?"

"Some . . . I guess. At least I thought so for a while, but lately . . ." He shrugged.

In a few minutes, Mrs. Catley announced that she had finished her work and it was time for them to go home. "I 'spect you'll be sleeping on that couch where Lawrence is, since Mr. Newman's got no other beds."

Once they were gone, I explored my uncle's house, which didn't take long because there were only the three rooms. Soon the tiredness of my trip drove me to the couch. I lay down for just a moment.

Bang! A door slammed shut, and I snapped awake. It was dark, and I couldn't remember where I was. Then an electric light snapped on, and a man's voice said, "Hey! Who are you, and what you doing in my house?"

It was my uncle. I was in California.

"Is that you, Jerry?"

I sat up and rubbed my eyes. "Yes, sir. I got in this afternoon, and Mrs. Catley let me in. I hope that was all right."

"Well, come over here, boy, and let me have a look at you in the light. I wasn't expecting you until tomorrow. How'd you find the house? My, you've grown. Last time I saw you, you were only . . . Oh. Sorry. Used to hate it when adults always commented on how much I'd grown, and here I'm doing it myself."

I went over to him. My uncle Thomas looked just like I had remembered him—tall, handsome, with a pencil-thin black mustache gracing the top of his lip. But he wasn't dressed like the Kodak picture sitting on Mama's dresser at home. Gone was the suit and matching fedora hat, pulled low over his left eye. There was no crisp dress shirt and paisley tie. Instead, he wore bib overalls over a faded red, long-sleeved undershirt. And his boots were all covered with the muck he must have been shoveling at the horse barn. If he was doing undercover work at the racetrack, guess he had to look the part. But to me he looked great!

"Welcome to California, Jerry!" he said, extending his hand just like I was a grown man meeting him for a business appointment. "Say, you want to go to work with me tomorrow? I might even be able to get you on for pay."

I guess I was grinning as though I was all teeth, but I couldn't help it. This was too good to be true, going on an undercover investigative assignment with my uncle.

"Will I meet any gangsters?"

He just cuffed the top of my head and then threw his arm around me as we headed for the kitchen. "You want something to eat?"

Chapter 5

The PRESS Pass

THE NEXT MORNING WAS SATURDAY, but I knew animals needed care seven days a week, so we left early for work in a fog so thick you could reach out and grab it by the handfuls. My uncle even walked down the street waving his hand as though he could shoo it away. Then he turned to me. "It gets this way sometimes early in the morning when the fog rolls in off the ocean, but it will probably burn off before ten o'clock."

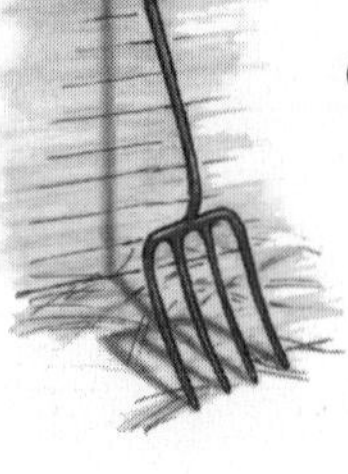

I pushed my tweed porkpie hat back on my head and drew in a deep breath through my nose. The air smelled damp but not thick like an east-Texas bayou with its swamp grass and mosquitoes and rotting logs. This was salty and a little sour. "Are we really close to the ocean?"

"Well, if you headed right on down Alvarado, you'd get to the sea in about thirteen miles, but Alvarado don't go through. Besides, we're going to take the streetcar only about four miles to Exposition Park."

When we got to the racetrack, Uncle Thomas talked to his boss. "I'll take responsibility for the boy. He'll work, or you don't have to pay him."

The boss chewed on his unlit cigar stub and took a step closer to me, huffing like a steam engine to move his enormous bulk. His watery blue eyes looked me up and down. He shrugged, and soon it was decided.

Before we began, Uncle Thomas introduced me to Mr. Catley, Lawrence's dad. Then he led me to the end of the long horse barn, where we set to work by ourselves cleaning out stalls and feeding the horses. The work was hard, and there wasn't much chance to talk most of the morning, but at one point I asked my uncle, "Does your boss have any idea why you are here?"

"I sure hope so," my uncle said with a crooked grin. "Because I'm not breaking my back for nothin', you know."

"But what if he's part of it?"

Leaning on his pitchfork, my uncle wiped the sweat off his brow. "Part of what?"

I looked around to make sure no one was near. "The crimes they're committin'," I whispered.

"Yeah, well, it sure is a crime how little they pay

us for all this hard work, but that's no secret," he said in a normal voice, shrugging off any concern that someone might overhear him. Then he looked at me with a deep frown that nearly brought his eyebrows together. "But . . . let's take a break."

We walked to the barn door and rolled it open on its overhead track. Uncle Thomas had been right; the sun was already out and the only trace of the fog was a few wispy clouds in the sky. We sat down on either side of the door with our backs to the barn poles.

"Now, tell me, what crime are *you* so worried about?" my uncle said, raising one eyebrow and leaning toward me with his best investigative-reporter squint.

I shook my head. "I don't know." But for no reason I could understand, my mind flashed back to lighting that fire under the church in east Texas. Did my mother tell him about what I'd done? I hadn't seen her telegram, but telegrams are expensive, and I doubted she would have wasted words explaining all that. I looked down at the dirt between my feet. I sure hoped my uncle didn't know about that fire.

Of course, I reassured myself, that's not what my uncle was asking. So I looked around again to make sure no one was near. "You're investigating crimes here at the racetrack, aren't you—for the newspaper?"

He laughed. "Investigating. . . ?" Then he glanced up and into the dark interior of the barn. "No, sir. There's nothing going on here but caring for horses.

I'm just trying to earn a little money to pay my many bills."

Before the words were out of his mouth, I smelled the stench of a cheap cigar and heard the wheezing of the boss man.

"Well, you boys—" he paused to suck air—"don't look like life's being too hard on you—" more air—"an' it's not going to be too hard on me, either, if I don't have to pay you . . . which I'm not going to do . . . if you don't get back to work . . . right now!"

We jumped up.

Uncle Thomas whipped his hat off his head. "Yes, sir. We already finished six stalls and were just taking a break, but we'll be heading back to work directly."

For the rest of the afternoon, I worried that I had ruined my uncle's investigation. I'd been in Los Angeles only one day, and already I was causing trouble.

"I didn't mean to get you in trouble with your boss," I said that evening as we rode home on the streetcar.

Uncle Thomas shook his head as though a gnat were buzzing in his ear. After a moment he spoke while he was still looking straight ahead. "There's no investigation, Jerry. I just work there."

"No investigation?" I waited a moment, then said, "But why were you so worried that your boss might hear?"

"If I was investigating him, I sure wouldn't want him to know—true enough. But I'm not. I just work there, so I don't want him *thinking* I'm investigating anything. He'd fire me for sure, and I need that job."

"Why? I thought you were a reporter. I thought you worked for the *Los Angeles Daily Times*."

"Ha!" He looked out the window at all the small houses and little corner stores we were passing. "Look, Jerry. I've written a few articles. Some of them have been printed, but I'm not on staff. I'm just a lowly stringer. Sure, I keep my eyes open for good stories and write them up from time to time. But they don't support me. Very few people at the paper even know who I am."

Well, I knew that to be true. Hardly anyone knew his name when I was trying to find him, and now he'd explained why.

"But you're a good writer," I said. "And you've done some important stories, like that one about the Stanley Steamer going 127 miles per hour."

"Did you think I wrote that?"

"Of course. You sent it to me, didn't you?"

"I just thought that a young boy like you would be interested in it. I had no idea you'd think I wrote it. I've never been to Florida, Jerry. I've never been near those speed-record time trials." He was quiet for a moment. Then he turned and looked at me. "I wish I had been there. That would have been something to see. I need a break like that so I could write a story they'd take notice of. I really need a break."

I just sat there in that streetcar looking down at

my dusty shoes. My uncle Thomas was not a famous reporter. He didn't even have a real job writing for the *Los Angeles Daily Times*. So if he wasn't a reporter, what chance was there for me to become one?

Finally my uncle gave me a shove with his elbow. "Hey, kid, don't look so glum."

Life in "L.A.," as I had learned to call it, fell into a routine: work at the stables, come home, eat, read, and bed. The only break was on the days when Mrs. Catley came over to clean and brought Lawrence. We got to be pretty good friends, and we'd talk about Texas or play checkers, but he didn't seem to be getting any better, and I started to worry that he might die.

Then on Monday, April 16, on the way home from work, Uncle Thomas said, "Hey, I got a lead on a story for the newspaper we might look into . . . maybe tomorrow evening. How 'bout that?"

The next day we hurried to finish our work early so we could get home. Uncle Thomas was going to take me somewhere, but he wouldn't tell me where. I imagined a concert or a stage show or something like that. I couldn't imagine what else might be happening in the evening. But when we got home, Uncle Thomas said I needed to get washed up and dressed in the clean shirt and pants he'd bought me.

The clothes he'd gotten me were secondhand, but at least they were clean. But when Uncle Thomas came out of his bedroom, I caught a whiff of bay rum aftershave. He stuck out his clean chin and stretched his neck as he straightened his black tie and tugged at the collar of a crisp yellow shirt. "How's that?" he asked and brushed a bit of unseen lint from his brown suit.

"Great."

He looked in the small mirror hanging by the door and set his sharp fedora hat on his head, pulling it low over his right eye and then swiping his finger along the brim. "Let's go get 'em!"

I had no idea where we were going, but when we caught the streetcar on First Street and headed back through downtown, I recognized many of the huge buildings I had seen on Friday. At first I thought we might be going to the newspaper office, but we kept on riding until we got off at San Pedro.

"Hey, we're almost to the train depot. Are we going somewhere, Uncle Thomas?"

"Not by train," he said, walking at a good clip. "We're going to church!" He turned and looked at me with a sly grin. "What do you think of that, Jerry? Think you can use a little church?"

A strange heat seemed to crawl up my neck and hide itself in the hair at the back of my head. Mama *must* have told him about me burning that church back in east Texas! How else could he know? But she couldn't have told him. I had to find out.

"Why we going to church?"

Uncle Thomas laughed. "Because . . . it's Sunday, and I haven't been to church in years." My pounding heart had just started to calm when he added, "And I'm sure it'll do you some good, too. You need it, boy!" He cuffed the top of my head, knocking off my pork-pie hat.

I caught it and put it back on. What did he mean, I *needed* church?

We walked on in silence until we came to a short little street called Azusa. At the end of the block, a crowd of people swarmed around a boxy building like bees at a hive. And parked out in the street were two shiny automobiles.

But if we were at church, it was the strangest church I'd ever seen. Someone had chopped off its peaked roof and replaced it with an ill-fitting flat one. Scars on the weathered siding in the shape of Gothic arches indicated that the doors and windows had been remodeled into rectangles; all, that is, except for one huge Gothic arch in front on the second floor. It still remained, looking like a doorway to thin air.

"This the church?" I asked.

Uncle Thomas was walking along with his head slightly down while he looked steadily from under the brim of his hat at the activity in the late-afternoon light. "They call it the Azusa Street Mission . . . supposed to be some kind of revival going on, people coming from everywhere. And with the looks of that new Packard and that Stanley Steamer parked out front, there's some mighty important people here tonight, too."

"Is *that* a Stanley Steamer?" My mouth gaped open. "You think it can go 127 miles per hour?"

"The one that set the record was probably a little more stripped down," he chuckled.

"That what you're goin' to write about? Do you think we could get a ride?"

"No, no," he said, stabbing his finger toward the building. "I want to know what's going on in *there*. There might be a real story here, after all."

I glanced back for one more look at the automobiles. "Yeah, but we'll never get in through this crowd," I said as we wove our way into its fringes.

Then I noticed something unusual: Black people and white people were mixed in together, making their way into the building. Then I saw some Chinese . . . and Mexicans . . . even some men with turbans on their heads. All in one place.

From inside the church, singing floated out through the open windows and doors, and some of the people in the crowd joined in.

Cupping his hand around his mouth so I could hear, Uncle Thomas said, "Don't give up too soon. We'll get through. Just stick close by and watch a pro work." He pulled a white card from his pocket and stuck it in the band around his hat. In large letters it said PRESS, and underneath, *Los Angeles Daily Times*.

He *was* a reporter after all!

I stayed right behind him as he pushed forward through the crowd, saying, "Excuse me! Excuse me! The *Daily Times*, coming through. Make way, please." And like water for a moving boat, people pressed aside to let us plow through.

Chapter 6

The Weird Babble of Tongues

UNCLE THOMAS'S METHOD got us through the crowd until we reached the open doors into the Azusa Street Mission.

"Make way, please. Excuse me."

But the singing was so loud, no one responded until Uncle Thomas resorted to tapping people on the shoulder and pointing to the press card on his hat. But we had moved inside only a short distance when a man with white gloves grabbed my uncle's fine fedora off his head and with a frown and a shake of his head handed it to him.

Before he could grab *my* hat, I snatched it off my head. I knew we shouldn't have been wearing our hats in a house of worship.

The singing rocked the church, but not with hymns I had ever heard. Accompanied only by a couple of tambourines, they flowed in a rhythmic and free form, sometimes following the familiar call and response by a strong-voiced person in the congregation. But sometimes words and harmonies wove together in a way that seemed . . . seemed somehow led by an unseen musician.

My uncle was continuing to move through the crowd. I followed but couldn't see his purpose until we reached a set of stairs that led up to the second floor. There were already people on the steps, but that's where Uncle Thomas wanted to be. Halfway up he stopped, and we turned around. Now we could see the whole room spread out before us.

In the center there was a makeshift pulpit that looked to me to be nothing but a couple packing crates with a cloth hung over it. Behind it were three chairs. In front of one chair was a black man, another an Asian, the third a white man.

I pulled on my uncle's arm and leaned close to him. "There's lots of white people in here." I didn't think my voice was loud enough for anyone else to hear, but the woman in front of us turned around and frowned. And she was white! But it was true. Though most were black, whites and Mexicans and other races were all mixed right in. I'd never seen such a thing before. Back in Texas whites went to one church and blacks went to theirs, and it was unthinkable to mix.

The singing went on until it was totally dark

outside, and I thought my legs were going to collapse. I couldn't imagine how some of the people could keep dancing through it all, raising their hands in worship and swaying from side to side. Occasionally people would break out in a "holy dance," and the others around them would move back a little to give them space.

The black man standing in front of one of the chairs behind the pulpit had been lifting both hands in worship and looking up as though he could see right through the ceiling. But then he dropped his gaze and looked around the room.

It was then that I noticed something strange about his left eye. It looked cloudy like a blue aggie marble. With his arms raised, he turned his hands over, palms down as though he were patting an unseen pillow. Slowly the singing quieted until there were just a few people here and there round the large room who continued humming their own soulful tunes as a kind of background music.

"Glory! . . . Glory! . . . Glory!" shouted the man as he moved up to the pulpit. Then, in a voice like a trumpet, he began . . .

"They once said nothing good could come out of Nazareth,
    But *Jesus* proved them wrong.
They expected a messiah from a rich and royal family,
    But *Jesus* was born in a manger.
They wanted a ruler who lived in a castle,

But *Jesus* had no place to lay his head.
They looked for a king on a horse like Caesar,
But *Jesus* came ridin' in on a donkey.

"That's right, now. That's right. You know it's right! And now . . .

"They're saying nothing good can come out of Los Angeles,
But look what God's been doin'.
They said no one would listen to an ol' black preacher,
But God's put *good news* in my mouth.
And gathered people from *every* tribe and *every* nation just to hear it.
They said God wouldn't visit a barn like this,
But His Holy Ghost has baptized us with fire.
And now we're smokin' like the incense in God's holy temple.

"Hallelujah! Hallelujah! Hallelujah!" The man swung his arms high and spun around as the crowd broke out in a roar of praise and clapping.

"That must be William Seymour," my uncle said, cupping his hand and speaking into my ear. "He's the pastor who pretty much started this whole thing."

Then the preacher bowed his head slightly and brought both hands together in front of his mouth as though he were praying. When the people had quieted, he continued. "Pentecost has surely come, and

with it the biblical evidences are following. People are being converted and sanctified and filled with the Holy Ghost, speaking in tongues as they did on that first Christian Pentecost.

"We started in a cottage prayer meeting at 214 Bonnie Brae Street, but God's work couldn't be contained there. So many people tried to pack into that poor house that the porch broke down under their weight.

"Now we've come here to revive this old church. It was abandoned as a house of worship years ago and turned into a warehouse, but God has restored it. Already thousands of people have received the message, and it is spreading across the land.

"Proud, well-dressed preachers come to 'investigate'—really, to find fault—but soon their high looks are replaced with wonder, then conviction comes, and often you will find them on their faces on the floor, asking God to forgive them and make them as little children."

While he was talking, I noticed an old black woman pushing her way through the crowd to get closer to the center. She hobbled along with the aid of one crutch, stopping every few moments to look around as though she was not sure where she was headed. But the people moved aside and allowed her through. When she arrived at the center where there was some open space, Pastor Seymour noticed her, but he kept talking while he watched her hobble over to him.

Finally he interrupted his message. "What is it, sister? What do you seek from the Lord tonight?"

She responded in a thin, high voice, "I just wanna walk right so I can serve da Lord and spread His Word."

"Do you believe in Jesus? Have you received the baptism with the Holy Ghost?"

She nodded her head deeply one time. "I believe, and I been water baptized, but I need da HOLY Ghos'," she said, with all her emphasis on *Holy*.

"Well, the Holy Ghost is always a gentleman," said the pastor. "He doesn't force himself on anyone, but He's no coward, either. He brings signs and gives gifts. Are you ready for that?"

Again she nodded deeply.

Pastor Seymour reached his hand out toward her and then turned his head to one side and tightly closed his eyes as he began to pray. I understood his first few words, but then something happened, and I couldn't recognize a word he said. It sounded like some kind of a foreign language.

While he prayed, the woman began bobbing her head up and down like a pigeon and rhythmically calling, "Jesus, Jesus, Jesus." Suddenly she shrieked and dropped her crutch, and the bobbing of her head turned into a sideways kind of hopping until that old woman was jumping up and down like a schoolgirl skipping rope. She wasn't crippled anymore.

Then as quickly as she had begun, she stopped, looked up at one of the bare light bulbs that hung from the ceiling, and began to speak with words I could not understand.

"She's speakin' in an unknown tongue," announced Pastor Seymour over her words. "Keep on, sister. Keep on."

While she spoke, a man standing along the far wall who appeared to be Mexican shouted, "Hallelujah, Jesus Christ, hallelujah!" and then was quiet.

When the woman finished, he again spoke, but with a very heavy accent. “Sir, that was not an unknown tongue. I am an Indian from central Mexico. Very few people know of my tribe, and I have never heard of a black person visiting us or learning our language, but that was my language, as clear as can be.”

William Seymour pointed at him. “What did she say, brother? What was God’s message?”

“She said . . . she told me to pray for a woman here. May I do that, Pastor Seymour?”

“By all means, brother. Let us not quench the Holy Ghost.”

“Oh no,” muttered my uncle. “This is too much.”

I turned toward him and must have had a frown of question marks all over my face, because he muttered, “All this could be faked, you know. How do we know that woman was crippled in the first place or that she was speaking some unknown Indian language?”

By this time, the Indian man was making his way through the crowd to a finely dressed man and woman standing arm in arm. In fact, the woman had a fur collar on her stylish coat. Maybe they had come in one of the automobiles.

“This is the woman I’m to pray for,” said the Indian man, looking back at Pastor Seymour.

“Do you have a special need, sister?” asked the black pastor.

She looked startled, but she said, “Yes, sir, I do. I have consumption so bad I can’t go anywhere without hanging on my poor husband’s arm.”

Pastor Seymour nodded toward the Indian man, who walked around behind the woman and put his hands on her back about shoulder high and then began to pray so quietly that I couldn't tell whether he was praying in English or Spanish or his native Indian language.

I looked at my uncle, and his mouth was literally hanging open as he stared at what was occurring. He must have sensed me watching him because, without taking his eyes off what was happening, he leaned toward me. "This is incredible. I've never seen anything like it in my life. Blacks and whites and Mexicans—or Indians—all together. That white woman actually allowing someone of color to touch her. This is a story, all right, a big story."

When the man had finished praying, he looked up and smiled at Pastor Seymour, and then he made his way back to where he had been standing.

"Well, sister?" said Pastor Seymour.

"Sister," whispered Uncle Thomas. "He called her sister."

A look came over the woman's face like she had tasted ice cream for the first time. "I can breathe. I am healed. I am healed!"

Suddenly an old black man with a strong but raspy voice began to sing:

> "Kind friends I want to tell you
>   because I love your soul.
> No doubt you been converted,
>   but have you ever been tol'.

Some people, they'll try an' fool you,
say there's nothing else to do.
But Jesus Christ my Savior,
He's got better things for you."

When he finished the verse, it seemed like everyone joined in on the chorus.

"He's got better things for you,
that none on earth can do.
He's got the Holy Ghost and fire,
that sure can see you through.
He's got better things for you,
that none on earth can do.
So place your mind on Jesus.
He's got better things for you."

The old man had started into a second verse when Uncle Thomas grabbed my arm. "Come on, let's go." But instead of guiding me down the steps and out of the building, he turned and led me up the stairs.

We entered a room as large as the one below from which the singing continued to rise. It was empty except for several groups of three or four chairs each. On the rough-board walls hung an array of canes, crutches, whiskey bottles, medicine bottles, and eyeglasses. It looked like some kind of a museum.

"Can I help you gentlemen?" It was the voice of a beautiful black woman who had come up behind us. "I'm Jennie Evans Moore," she explained as she extended her hand to Uncle Thomas.

"What's been happening here?" Uncle Thomas said, pointing at the floor and making a face like he had eaten something sour. "Are you part of this . . . this . . . whatever it is?"

"Yes, I'm part of this Pentecostal movement, and what you've seen for yourself is probably the best explanation for what's happening." Her voice rose as the sentence ended as though she were asking a question.

"Well?" He looked around the room. "And all of these?"

"This used to be the sanctuary of the old church, but it wouldn't be safe for such large crowds. We're all for Holy Ghost fire, but we wouldn't want people to get trapped if this place burned down."

I shuddered as an image flashed before my eyes of the fire I'd set back in Romburg. What if people had been trapped in that church as it went up in flames? Without realizing it I muttered out loud, "Oh, thank you, Jesus."

"Oh, that's right, young man. 'O give thanks unto the Lord, for he is good: for his mercy endureth for ever.' Psalm 107 and 1." She smiled at me and then looked back at Uncle Thomas. "Now we use this for a prayer and deliverance room." She gestured around the room with a slim and refined hand. "These trophies you see mounted on the wall? They were captured from the devil. We keep them here to remind us how very good God is."

"Trophies, huh? From people who got healed?"

said Uncle Thomas.

Miss Moore nodded.

"Then I suppose you'll be mounting that crutch, or is that the one you use over and over again?"

With sharpness in her voice, Miss Moore said, "There's nothing fake about the goodness of the Lord!"

"Then why isn't your reverend's glass eye up here on the wall? Doesn't he have enough faith to be healed?"

"It's not a glass eye," she said crisply. "He simply lost the sight in it when he suffered smallpox. But the Lord used it to call him into the ministry. So, 'all things work together for good to them that love God, to them who are the called according to his purpose.' Romans 8 and 28."

"Hmm," my uncle mused as though he were considering her response. "How late will this go on tonight?"

Miss Moore shrugged. "As long as the Spirit moves—midnight, maybe later."

Uncle Thomas put his hat on, making sure that Miss Moore couldn't miss seeing his press card. "Well, I think we've stayed late enough. Come on, Jerry."

We went back down the stairs and were working our way through the crowd, when Uncle Thomas stopped to listen while a large white man addressed the people.

"Ladies and gentlemen," he said in a resonant voice. "My name is Gold, and I am a Jewish rabbi. . . ."

"Now I've heard everything," muttered my uncle.

"I want to give praise to God tonight for miraculously healing me and showing me that Jesus is my Messiah." Gold stopped for a moment, as if unsure whether to proceed.

"I have a prophecy from the Holy Ghost, if you'll permit me, Pastor Seymour." He waited, and when William Seymour nodded toward him and extended an open hand of permission, the man continued. "I received a vision in which I saw the people of California living as sinfully as in the days of Noah until God brought a great destruction upon them, crushing everything, knocking our great buildings to the ground, setting flame to the city. Oh, brothers and sisters, spread the word so we might come to repentance and avoid this terrible punishment."

I saw Uncle Thomas roll his eyes. Now he'd heard everything.

Chapter 7

Shake, Rattle, and Roll

WHEN WE LEFT THE STRANGE CHURCH, there were still people crowded around outside trying to hear what was happening. As we walked down the dark street, we could still hear the fading lines of the song they had taken up again.

> "He's got better things for you,
> that none on earth can do.
> He's got the Holy Ghost and fire,
> that sure can see you through."

My uncle's voice sounded as close and soft as the velvety night when he said, "It's a good thing there aren't any houses next door. People might not take too kindly to all that noise carrying on till midnight every night."

He was right. A lumberyard on one side, a tombstone shop on the other, and a horse stable on a third were what surrounded the old whitewashed building—none likely to complain. "But do they do it every night?" I asked.

"That's what I understand . . . and who knows how long it will continue?"

When we got home, Uncle Thomas sat down at his little desk and turned on his green-shaded lamp. "You think you can go to sleep there on the couch while I type this up?"

I nodded and unfolded the old quilt I'd been using, then sat down to remove my shoes and get ready for bed. But I really wanted to watch my uncle write his story. That's the part that interested me most. How was he going to turn our evening into a newspaper story?

Once he had rolled a sheet of paper into his little typewriter and began to peck away at the keys, I slipped over behind him in my bare feet and read over his shoulder.

Weird Babel of Tongues

New Pentecost Is Breaking Loose
Wild Scene Last Night on Azusa Street
Strange Languages Spoken

Breathing strange utterances and

```
mouthing a creed, which it would seem
no sane mortal could understand, the
newest religious sect has started in
Los Angeles. Meetings are held in a
tumbled-down shack on Azusa Street,
near San Pedro Street, and the devo-
tees—
```

My uncle's head turned around. "Hey, I thought you were in bed. What are you still doing up?"

"I just wanted to see what you were writing."

"You'll see it tomorrow. Now, get to bed." He turned back and started to type but then stopped. "By the way, when I finish this, I'm going to run it over to the *Times*. So if you wake up and I'm not here, I'll be back before too long."

I tried to stay awake, but soon the irregular snapping of the typewriter put me to sleep.

A crash from the kitchen woke me. It was still completely dark. Something else crashed, shattering glass this time. I jumped off the couch and started toward the kitchen, then had a terrible thought: What if a burglar was in there? But before I could stop, I bumped into the doorjamb like a drunken person weaving from side to side. What was wrong? I couldn't even walk straight.

"Uncle Thomas?"

"Yeah . . . yeah. Hold on, Jerry. Don't go in the

kitchen till we get a light on. You might cut your feet . . . I heard something break."

In a moment he switched on the lights, first in his bedroom and then in the kitchen. Everything seemed normal again—no burglar—but a pot had fallen off the edge of the stove and a glass pitcher had fallen from the shelf and broken on the floor.

"What did that?" I asked, half expecting my uncle to tell me his house was haunted by ghosts.

"I think you just experienced your first earthquake. But it was just a little one. They happen all the time out here. You'll get used to them." He started to pick up the glass. "I shouldn't have left that pitcher on the shelf. I was just asking for trouble. Now, you go on an' get back to bed, get some more sleep."

I yawned. "What time is it, Uncle Thomas?"

"Just past five. It's not time to get up yet."

On our way to work at the racetrack that morning, Uncle Thomas picked up the early edition of the morning paper and flipped through it while we rode on the streetcar.

"Here it is." He stabbed the paper with his finger and held it over where I could see. "Here's my article. Ha, ha! They printed it! 'New sect of fanatics is breaking loose' and '*Gurgle* of wordless talk by a sister.' . . . Oh no, oh *no*! They butchered it all up. Listen to this . . . 'Colored people and a *sprinkling* of whites compose the congregation, and night is made *hideous* in the neighborhood by the *howling* of the worshipers.' " Uncle Thomas looked disgusted. "I didn't write it like that! I said, 'Both colored and white people worshiped together until late into the night.' "

He stopped and folded the paper while he stared straight ahead. "You know what? They might have faked the talking in tongues—or whatever they call it—and they might have faked the healings, but there's one thing they couldn't have faked." He stopped and turned to me as though I knew what that was.

I just stared back, waiting for him to explain.

"Different races mixing together—blacks and whites and everybody. That just doesn't happen on its own! I was thinking about that all night. That's more of a miracle than anything else. Something's going on there."

He returned to reading the article. "Let's see . . . Oh, here we go. 'They spend hours swaying forth and back in a nerve-racking attitude of prayer and supplication. They claim to have "the gift of tongues," and to be able to comprehend the babel.

" 'Such a startling claim has never yet been made by any company of fanatics'—I didn't write *fanatics*—'even in Los Angeles, the home of almost numberless creeds.' " He stopped reading word for word and mumbled as he scanned on down the article. "Uh-oh, here we go again, 'Clasped in his big fist the colored brother holds a miniature Bible from which he reads at intervals, one or two words—never more.'

"I didn't write it that way," said Uncle Thomas, shaking his head.

"What did you say?"

"I just said something about his sermon not being boring. They twisted it all around. I'll admit that I have my questions. I don't know if what we saw last night was for real or not, but I didn't write it to make Seymour look like a fool."

He went back to the paper. " 'After an hour spent in exhortation, the brethren present are invited to join in a meeting of prayer, song, and testimony. Then it is that pandemonium breaks loose, and the bounds of reason are passed by those who are "filled with the spirit," whatever that may be.' Well, I did write that. Do you think that's disrespectful, Jerry? I don't."

"It sounds," I began. "Well, it sounds . . ."

"Oh no! Listen to this paragraph . . .

> " 'You-oo-oo gou-loo-loo come under the bloo-oo-oo boo-loo,' shouts an old colored 'mammy' in a frenzy of religious zeal. Swinging her arms wildly about her, she continues with the strangest harangue ever uttered. Few of her words are intelligible, and for the most part her testimony contained the most outrageous jumble of syllables, which are listened to with awe by the company."

Uncle Thomas smacked the newspaper with his hand. "I feel like giving up as a reporter if they're going to hack my work apart like that."

But by then we had arrived at our stop for the racetrack, and we got off the streetcar. All the way to the boss man's office, my uncle walked along with a frown, not saying a word.

Inside the office, the boss swung his feet down off his desk and pulled his cigar from his mouth like a cork from a medicine bottle. "You boys just do the basics this morning and then come on back up here to the office. I've got somethin' else in mind for you when you're finished."

The morning passed in sullen silence without us talking except to do our work. But I really wanted to know what my uncle thought about what we'd seen the night before. He had seemed skeptical, questioning whether the miracles and the "tongues" were real, so why was he so upset that his article seemed to ridicule William Seymour and his Azusa Street Mission?

We were cleaning out the stall of a big bay when I finally just blurted it right out.

Uncle Thomas was silent for so long that I thought I'd made him mad. Then he said, "It's like family. You might fight all the time at home with your brothers and sisters, but if someone else attacks one of you, you all stick together. Yeah, I had my questions, even wove 'em into my article—but it was the editors who rewrote it to ridicule. That's not the way I wrote it."

"But why would they do that?"

"Huh! If you asked them, they'd probably say that it sells more papers . . . but I think there's another reason." Uncle Thomas leaned on his pitchfork and frowned. "Has to do with crossing the color line. They have to make the whole thing look foolish or they'd have to face the biggest miracle of all—blacks and whites worshiping *together*. White people respecting a black man enough to accept him as their leader. Now, *that's* just not acceptable. Down deep, most white people don't think a black man ever knows more than they do."

He pitched four big forkfuls of fresh straw into the stall before he continued. "Know what, Jerry? They cut out my whole section about that Indian man putting his hands on that fancy white woman's shoulders and praying for her. Don't know whether she was really healed, but him touching her and the idea that God might work through *him* to help *her*—that'd be more than most white people can stomach."

"You think that's why they cut it out?" I asked.

"Yep!" He led the sleek bay thoroughbred back into her stall, then came out and put his hands on his hips. "But you know what? They didn't cut that prophecy of some awful destruction coming." He grinned. "That should be some kind of test for what's real."

About ten o'clock we finished with the basic work and returned to the office. We hadn't taken a break all morning, but my uncle wanted to find out what the boss man wanted us to do next. "We can get a little break when we know," he said.

The boss was reading the newspaper when we walked in. Uncle Thomas stared at the front page facing us. "Is that today's paper?"

The boss squinted at the top of the paper. "April 18, 1906. Sounds like today to me."

"But . . . where did you get it?"

The boss man's eyes narrowed. "You can be sure I didn't steal it from you!" He tucked his double chin indignantly. "Got it from the boy on the corner not ten minutes ago. But you better watch your tone of voice, boy, or you'll be walking the street lookin' for another job. You got that?"

"I'm sorry . . . sir," said my uncle. "Just noticing that headline. Must be a later edition than I got this morning."

Then I saw it. The five-inch-tall headline blazed: "SAN FRANCISCO LEVELED."

"Oh, this?" The boss turned the paper over and looked at the front page. "Yep, shake, rattle, and roll! Big earthquake hit Frisco last night. Whole city has been wiped out according to this. Says here it happened at 5:13 A.M."

My jaw dropped. That was when we had heard glass breaking in my uncle's kitchen!

My uncle bit his lower lip and frowned like he was adding up a column of numbers. "Boss," he said suddenly, "we're quitting. Wonder if you could pay us, and we'll be on our way."

"Wait a minute! You can't just quit like that. I got work for you to do this afternoon."

What was my uncle doing? Two days earlier, he'd said that he needed this job just to put bread on his table. Now he was walking out in the middle of the morning just because he'd seen a new edition of the newspaper!

"I'm sorry," my uncle said, "but I've got somethin' I've gotta do for the next few days, and it can't wait. Could you get us our money?"

The boss man glared at both of us. "That go for you, too, boy?"

I looked at my uncle, not knowing what to say, but he answered for me. "Figure it does." He took off his hat and wiped the backside of his arm across his sweaty forehead. "Jerry'll be heading home, so you better pay him, too."

Home? What was going on?

Huffing and puffing, the boss rose from his chair. "I've a mind to confiscate your pay for not giving me notice," he said, heading for a small closet in the corner of the office. He came back and slapped a few dollar bills on the table, not even taking time to count it out for us. "Don't expect to get another job here or with anyone I know! Ya hear?"

"Thank you." Uncle Thomas took the money and turned for the door while I just stood there. "Come on, Jerry. Let's go," he said, grabbing my arm.

We walked fast, all the way to the streetcar line, before I said, "I didn't like that guy, but I didn't think he was all *that* bad."

Stepping onto the running board of the streetcar before it had even come to a stop, Uncle Thomas grinned. "Oh, it wasn't the boss. It was that newspaper he was holding. I just got my big break!"

We slid into our seats. "What do you mean?"

"The earthquake! If that headline is right, there's a big, big story in San Francisco, and I'm heading there quick as I can to report on it."

Something was troubling me. "Wait. When you said I was going home, did you mean your house or are you sending me back to Texas?"

"Texas, of course. I'll be heading up to San Francisco, and it's a disaster area, like a war zone. I can't have a kid along." He looked at me and then waved his hand. "Ah, Jerry, don't be so upset. We've had a good time together, but now . . . now I've got things I gotta do, and I can't be taking care of you."

I looked down at the floor. "Didn't know I was that much trouble," I mumbled. Thoughts of Texas raced through my mind. Guess I was a lot of trouble after all. That's why Mama sent me to "the end of the earth," and now that was why Uncle Thomas was sending me back. But I really didn't want to go. I wanted to go to San Francisco. *That* sounded like the *real* end of the earth, especially if the whole city had been smashed—kind of like the end of the *world*.

Finally Uncle Thomas said, "Tell you what. Let's go home and get changed, and then I'll take you over to the newspaper office while I find out what's actually going on up in Frisco. Maybe this isn't such a big deal after all. I'll think about it . . . I'll think about it, all right?"

At home, I washed and changed as quickly as I could, hoping to show Uncle Thomas that I wouldn't be any hindrance to him. I could use the money I had earned at the racetrack to pay my way, but I knew even that wouldn't be enough. I had to prove myself valuable to him before he'd have reason to take me with him.

Chapter 8

Assignment: The End of the Earth

AT QUARTER TILL NOON when we walked into the newspaper office, teletype machines were clattering at full speed, and Mr. Garrison, the city editor I remembered from a few days ago, was reading various facts to some of the reporters and office workers who were standing around—I spotted Miss Tulip-Lips among them.

Squinting through his half-moon glasses, Mr. Garrison read, " 'Hundreds, perhaps thousands, are trapped in the rubble. . . . Serious aftershocks continue to do more damage. . . . Fires are burning out of control. . . . In Santa Cruz County a whole section of forest has been leveled. . . . Cracks are opening in the ground without notice, causing panic among people who fear falling in.' "

He stopped reading aloud and scanned the reports in his hand. "Oh, here's a comforting thought." His eyebrows arched high. " 'Scientists are speculating whether this is just the first of a series of quakes going up and down the coast. A major aftershock struck at 8:14 A.M. and caused the collapse of many damaged buildings. If these quakes produce a domino effect, damage may be worse in L.A. because of the convergence of major fault lines here. There's even talk of the whole California coast breaking off into the Pacific Ocean.' "

He looked around the room. "This could be the biggest story of the century. We've got to get someone up there right now!"

"I can go," said my uncle Thomas. We were standing at the edge of the little group.

A couple of people looked at him, and Mr. Garrison also glanced his way; then his eyes kept roving. "Jack? Where's Jack? Can he go?"

In a whiny voice, Miss Tulip-Lips said, "He's sick today, Mr. Garrison. Real sick, his wife says."

"What about you, Roger? Can you drop that city hall story and head on up there?"

"I don't know, Mr. Garrison. I've been working for three weeks to get an interview with the mayor, and he's agreed to meet with me this afternoon. This city hall thing could be a big story, and I'd hate to miss it."

"Yeah, yeah. Well, who else can we send?"

No one answered for several moments, and then my uncle raised his hand. "Like I said, sir, I'm available. All I need is a press camera!"

The editor studied my uncle over the tops of his glasses like this was the first time he had seen him. "All right, Newman. You leave immediately. But you better get us a story. I want you to report back three times a day. A lot of the telegraph and telephone lines are down, but that's your problem. I want copy on my desk, and lots of it."

He grinned wryly. "What was that you wrote about that strange church last night—some guy prophesying destruction? Now, there's an angle: 'Prophet Foretold Frisco Quake!' or 'End of Earth Begins in S.F.' You think those headlines would sell papers?"

My uncle looked like he was going to answer, but suddenly there was a rumbling and a rattling like a train was coming through the office. Miss Tulip-Lips began to scream, and others joined with her. "It's a quake," yelled Mr. Garrison as he fell to the floor and began to crawl. "Get under your desks, and don't panic. Don't panic, people. Don't panic."

"Come on," Uncle Thomas said, grabbing my arm. "The hallway's safer."

By the time we got there, the earthquake had stopped, and the only effect on the newspaper office was some lights hanging from the ceiling that were still swinging back and forth a little.

"Safest place in an earthquake," explained Uncle Thomas quickly as he looked around at the walls and ceiling, "is in a hallway or a doorway. The closer the walls are to you, the more support there is around you and the less chance for something to cave in on you." By then the lights had stopped swinging, and all seemed quiet, but he kept talking. "And never run outside, because in California, the first thing likely to happen is for those red tiles to slide off the roof. 'Course, this big building doesn't have tiles on the roof, but it's something to look out for."

Everything had happened so fast that I hardly had time to be afraid, but then it struck me that Uncle Thomas had been chattering faster than an angry squirrel. He didn't look scared, and he hadn't acted scared like that editor, but he wasn't entirely calm, either.

Right then I decided I'd rather face a tornado. At least, if you were looking, you could see it coming.

Finally Uncle Thomas said, "I think everything's quiet." He led me down a hall to a room where he checked out a camera and got several rolls of film.

I didn't say anything as we went out and climbed on the streetcar and headed for home. My uncle was getting ready to go on the biggest news assignment of his life, but I was being sent back to Texas. I had to think of a reason why he should take me with him to San Francisco!

"Uncle Thomas, with that camera and all your luggage, you're going to need someone to help you carry things. Maybe I could do that for you."

He just gave me a frown like I didn't know what I was talking about.

When we got off the streetcar and began walking toward his house, I tried again. "What if I can't get a train ticket back to Texas today? Then can I come with you?"

His pace didn't even slow. "If there's any problem, I'll leave you with Mrs. Catley. She can put you on the train tomorrow or the next day—whenever you can get a ticket."

Usually I'm good at talking people into doing what I want, but I couldn't think of a thing that would convince my uncle to take me to San Francisco. Try as I did, I couldn't stop the tears building up in my eyes. The sidewalk in front of me began to get blurry, and I wiped first one eye and then the other with my wrists, trying to make my action casual so my uncle wouldn't see it. We were almost to his house, and I couldn't think of a thing to do or say.

"But I burned that church, Uncle Thomas," I blurted out. "I can't go back home."

He stopped cold, right there on the street. "You *what*?"

"You know, I burned down that church, an' . . . if I go home, I'll be in big trouble."

"What in blazes are you talking about, son?"

I held my breath. Was it possible that he didn't know? "I . . . didn't Mama tell you in the telegram about me getting in trouble? About me lighting that fire?"

"She didn't tell me anything but that she wanted you to come and stay with me for a while. Now, what's all this talk about you burning a church?"

I felt relief like I'd just stepped out of a smokehouse. He hadn't known after all. Suddenly more tears were coming to my eyes, and I had to look away from him as I spoke. "I didn't mean to do it. It was an accident. . . ." And suddenly I was telling him the whole thing.

When I finished, he just threw his arm around my shoulder and walked me into the house without speaking. I felt even more relieved at having told him. No matter what happened now, some kind of big wall between us had come down.

"Go on into the kitchen and get yourself a drink of water and wash your face," he said, his voice unusually husky and deep.

When I returned, he was sitting in his chair by his little desk. He had hung his hat on one finger and was aimlessly twirling it around and around. I sat down on the couch opposite him, not knowing what else to do. Finally he said, "I remember being in trouble when I was about your age. Fact is, I've made plenty of trouble for myself since then, too. Right off, I don't know how you should handle your problem back in Texas, but I can see that we don't have to figure it out today. So pack your things. We're going to San Francisco. We'll figure out Texas later."

When we got to the train depot an hour later, the place was swarming with people like ants at a picnic.

"What's the big occasion?" I asked a kid about my age who was struggling to carry two big suitcases and keep up with his parents and two younger sisters.

"We're getting out of here," he said. "We're not waiting till California falls into the ocean."

I looked at my uncle. "Did you hear that?"

"Yeah, well, we shouldn't have any trouble going north if everyone else is trying to go east." He was craning his neck from side to side to see what ticket line was shortest.

Getting on a train north was the easy part, and for the first few hours north, it moved smoothly, but then we began slowing down for miles at a time. And sometimes we stopped in the middle of nowhere and sat for fifteen minutes. At one of the stops, my uncle told me to stay put while he got up and headed forward into the car ahead of us.

When he returned, I said, "What's going on? Why are we stopped?"

"It's just a little bridge. They're worried that the earthquake might have damaged it, so before they take the train across, they send someone underneath the bridge to see if it's safe."

I gulped. I hadn't thought about the train dropping off a bridge.

We got over the bridge all right, but by late afternoon, our delays were more frequent, and Uncle Thomas again went to see why. When he came back he explained that now they had to be careful of curves. They were afraid the tracks might have separated in some places, and we could be derailed.

"Are we the first train through?"

"No, but the aftershocks continue to do more damage."

The more time that passed, the more frustrated my uncle became. "I need to be in San Francisco *now* if I'm going to report on this disaster, not tomorrow or the next day."

But it was noon the next day before we arrived in Oakland, as close as we could get by train. Miles earlier we had begun seeing evidence of damage. Buildings had huge cracks going from the ground up, and whole walls that had fallen away, exposing the rooms inside like a child's dollhouse. Sides of hills had slid down, burying houses and roads.

But Oakland was a different story. Not only was there lots of damage to many buildings, but the city seemed packed with refugees—people who had fled across the bay from San Francisco, but also people from Oakland who didn't dare return to their damaged homes.

In a small park near the train station, several people were spread out like picnickers at a crowded beach, and Uncle Thomas went up to one man who was trying to create a makeshift tent out of blankets. "Do you folks live in San Francisco?"

The man glanced at us while stringing a rope between one tree and another. "We did until yesterday." His wife was sitting on a crate, holding a young girl on her lap. They stared at us with vacant eyes and open mouths.

"I'm from the *Los Angeles Daily Times*," Uncle

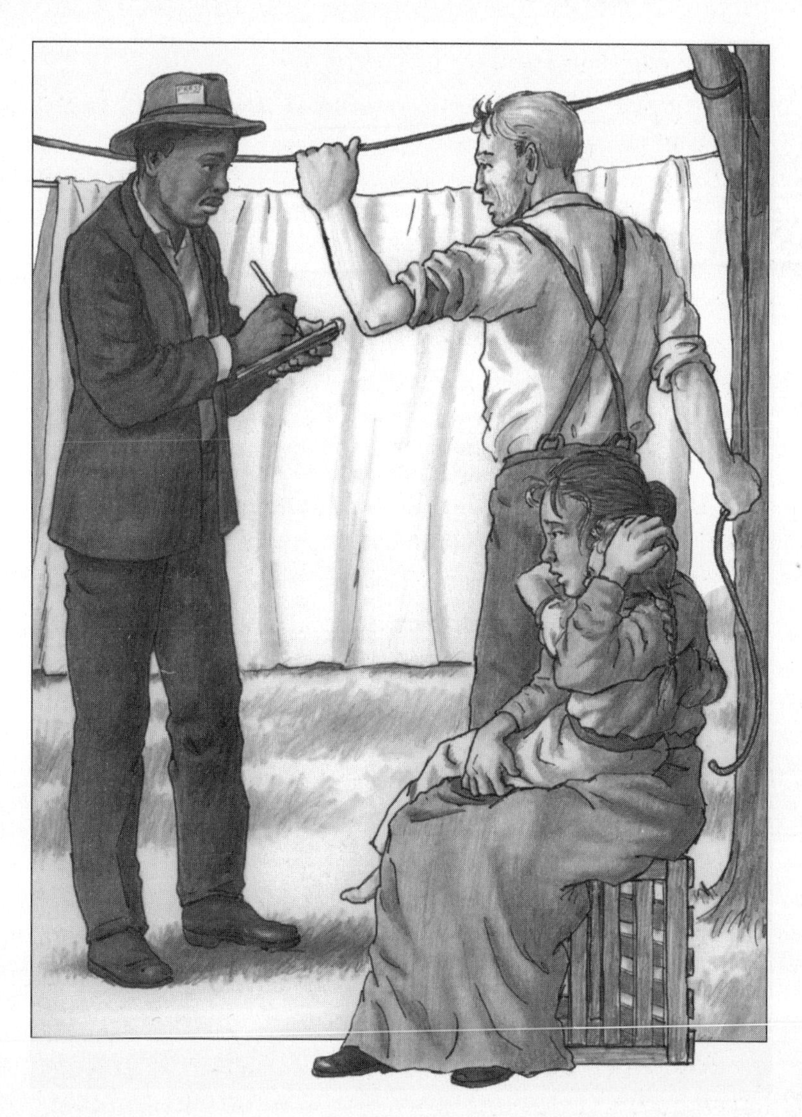

Thomas said, adjusting his press card in the front of his hat and poising his pencil over his notebook. "Could you tell me what it was like when the earthquake hit?"

"What it was like?" The man gave us a sour frown. "Nothing human words could describe. I was a wealthy man before I got out of bed yesterday. Now all I own is what you see here and two lots piled with rubble—one where our home stood, and one where my business stood."

"But what was it like?"

The man stopped adjusting the rope and stood openmouthed like he was trying to remember something from a former age. "I had just poured a cup of coffee and had walked into the living room, when I heard this loud rumbling coming from the west. Suddenly the house began to shake. Most of the plaster in the dining room fell from the ceiling. Furniture—our piano, bookcases, sofa, and chairs—danced across the living room as though possessed with demons. The doors of our cabinets popped open, and the china and crystal rained down from both sides of the kitchen as though imps were in the cabinets throwing our dinnerware across the kitchen at each other.

"It went on and on forever, it seemed, and then ended with a huge bang like some kind of an explosion.

"For a moment everything was silent—except for the water in the bathroom. One of our water pipes broke, and water was spraying everywhere. Then my wife and daughter began to scream."

He looked at us as though unable to believe what he was saying. "I actually was glad to hear them screaming. It meant that they were alive." He looked down. "I cut my feet running over broken glass to get to their rooms."

Uncle Thomas was writing furiously in his little notebook.

Finally the man said, "Is that what you needed to know?" It was as though he thought Uncle Thomas was some kind of an official whom he had to answer.

"Yes, thank you. Would you mind if I took a picture of you and your family?"

As Uncle Thomas prepared his camera, the man turned back to building his shelter. He did not answer one way or the other about the picture. But as Uncle Thomas stepped back and prepared to snap a picture of the man with his wife and child, the man said, "Actually, our house wasn't damaged too badly, but the fire came up the street and took every house on the block."

As we walked away, Uncle Thomas said to me, "We've got to get over to San Francisco. Let's go find the ferry."

While we waited for the anxious refugees to get off the ferry so we could get on board, we watched the angry columns of black smoke rising from the city on the other side of the bay. Shining through the smoke, the setting sun turned the whole sky into churning black, red, and orange. Once we were on board and underway, there was no way to turn back. I shuddered. I was either heading to the end of the earth or into the gates of hell itself.

As the ferry nosed into the dock on the other side, we could hardly get off for the flood of people trying to get on. We started up Market Street, but could see nothing had been done to clean up the city. Everywhere we looked fires still raged, creating their own wind. The city was literally being eaten up in a fire storm that jumped from building to building and across alleys and streets.

The streets were humped into ridges and depressions, and piled with the debris of fallen walls. The steel rails of San Francisco's cable cars were twisted into jagged angles, perpendicular to the street in places. A great water main had burst, boiling water from the middle of the street like an artesian fountain. At another point the street just ended in a cliff only to continue on at a level five feet below.

"Here," said Uncle Thomas, "you take pictures while I take notes. You know how to use a camera?"

I shook my head no, almost incapable of talking in the middle of such a disaster. He showed me the trigger and how to look through the viewfinder. "When I tell you to, you snap pictures, okay?"

As we picked our way along through the rubble toward the heart of the city, Uncle Thomas pointed one direction and then another, instructing me to take pictures. Here and there through the smoke, creeping warily under the shadows of tottering walls, emerged men and women. It was like meeting the handful of survivors after a great war. They carried blankets and other possessions to any open space that would now be safe, whether it had once been a park or a vacant lot. There they made camps around bonfires and talked in low tones.

As we came around the one remaining wall of a shattered building, Uncle Thomas pointed down the street and said, "There, get a picture of that!"

"What is it?"

"The shattered dome of the City Hall."

Most of the stone had been shaken from the great dome, leaving standing the naked framework of steel like the skeleton of a gigantic monster. As we approached, we discovered that the pillars that had adorned the front of the building had fallen out into the street, where they shattered into wheels like giant carrots sliced by a chef.

I felt numb. The destruction just went on and on. Finally we were walking through streets lighted only by the fires that still burned in various buildings.

"Uncle Thomas," I finally ventured, "where are we going to sleep tonight?"

His eyes were glazed, and he looked around like he was lost. "Guess we'll have to ask some of these poor people to let us share their campfire. Don't dare take shelter inside one of these damaged buildings. The slightest aftershock could bring any one of them down on our heads!"

Chapter 9

Return to Azusa

BOOM! *BOOM! BOOM!* A series of teeth-jarring blasts ripped the night.

I sat up from the damp ground where I had finally fallen asleep under a thin blanket. "What was that?"

Most of the refugees in the little group we had joined didn't even stir with the explosions, but an old man who, in the flickering firelight, looked like a gold miner was awake. Under a floppy hat, a toothless grin split his huge black beard that grew almost up to his eyes. "Oh, they jist tryin' to blow out them fires so they can save th' rich people's homes, but it ain't worked yet. You cain't stop the Lord's judgment with dynamite, you know."

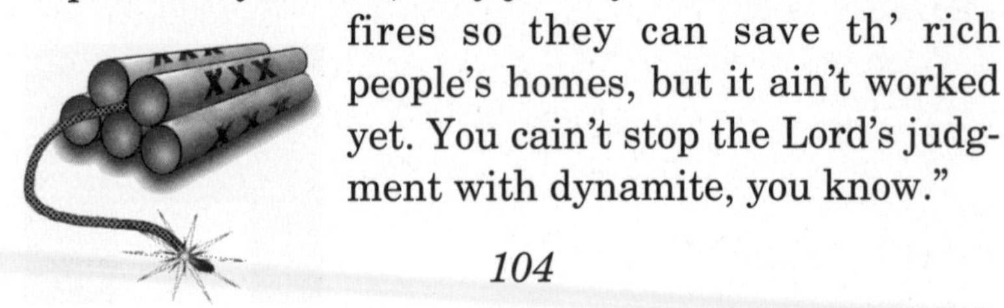

"Dynamite?" said Uncle Thomas, sitting up and rubbing his head. "What are they doing with dynamite?"

"Blowin' up buildings in the path of the fire so when it gits there it won't have anything to burn. That's how they hope to stop it. But . . ." He raised his eyebrows like they were a cat's toy on a string and shrugged.

We lay back down, but in my mind I kept seeing buildings being blown to bits to starve the fiery dragon in its black tracks. In the end, it all merged into a dream in which it was the little church in Romburg that blew up to keep me from burning it down. After the explosion, I was left standing in the pine woods with my cattail torch in hand while all the people paraded past me looking and shaking their heads like I was a disgraceful museum exhibit.

I woke up exhausted and aching and troubled in my spirit over the dream.

Day was trying to dawn through the smoky gloom. A sickly light crept over the ruins as the churning sky above pulsed and fluttered between gray and lavender. Then it turned to mauve and yellow and very dreary. There was no sun, and I felt just about like the day looked.

"Want some of this here roast beef?"

I sat up and looked over at the prospector, who seemed to be the only other person in camp. He sat on a wooden box, using a large hunting knife to carve bites of meat off a dripping roast he held in his left hand.

"Where'd you get that?" I asked.

"Down on Market Street. Whole string of dead steers are lined up in the middle of the street. The quake must've killed 'em, and the fire pretty much roasted 'em. I don't know who dragged 'em out into the street. But I reckon the meat ought to be good for a couple more days . . . 'less it turns hot." With the greasy hand in which he held his hunting knife, he pointed at me and said, "Want a bite?"

I shook my head.

"Yeah. Well, your partner didn't, neither. Guess he's gone off to find more civilized victuals. He better take care, though. I warned him. Mayor's issued a shoot-to-kill order for anyone caught lootin'. They already shot three young fellers yesterday, shot 'em down without mercy, they did. But I figgered this beef is fair for the pickin's, seein' as how it was right out there in the middle of the street." He stuffed the bite into his mouth and chewed hard for a moment. "Come to think of it, it's kinda tough. Might be horse. Never did look at the hooves."

I got up and rolled my blanket, fixin' to find Uncle Thomas before I threw up.

"Say," said the prospector, "you wouldn't call what I did lootin', now, wouldja?"

"Whadd'ya mean?"

"You know, helpin' myself to a little breakfast."

I shrugged. "How would I know?"

"Heh, heh, I figgered if anybody knows, you colored boys would know what you can get away with."

I felt like punching him in the face. "I don't loot or steal," I growled and walked away so I wouldn't do something stupid. How *dare* he think I was such a lowlife just because of the color of my skin? *He* was the one out looting. I came from a good family. I wasn't a criminal. . . . And then somewhere in the back of my mind a little whisper teased, *Except for burning down churches!*

I found Uncle Thomas a block away, coming down the street toward me with a big grin on his face and a package under his arm.

"You won't believe it, Jerry! Right around that corner, there's a man with a deli, and he's open for business. Brick buildings on both sides of him are badly damaged, but his little frame storefront suffered nothing more than some broken windows and a jammed door. Oh yeah, his chimney fell down. He lives in back and said he had to be in his shop to watch over things. He was just sweeping up some of the mess. Here, look at this."

My uncle unwrapped a loaf of bread—a little hard—and a hunk of cheese, and then from his pockets he began pulling oranges and apples. "Pretty good, huh?"

We found a place to sit and eat our breakfast, and then Uncle Thomas said our next job was to send a report back to the newspaper. Immediately after the quake, telephone and telegraph connection between San Francisco and the rest of the world had been completely cut off. Then a telegraph line to Hawaii began to work. Several hours later a line to Oakland was restored.

By noon that Friday, four wires had been restored. We had to wait three hours for our turn to send a report to Los Angeles. He parked me in the line to hold a place and kept disappearing, tracking down more facts. When he came back he was shaking his head. "City officials are saying that the earthquake and fires together have claimed the lives of more than three thousand people and over twenty-eight thousand buildings! What happened here is one of the most devastating natural disasters in world history."

Uncle Thomas finally got his story through. Within half an hour, a brief response came, written in that strange style of telegraph messages—all capital letters and no punctuation, only the word *STOP* for the end of sentences:

> **GREAT STORY STOP RETURN WITH PICTURES ASAP STOP**

Train service had finally been restored up the western side of the bay right into the southern part of San Francisco itself, but it wasn't so easy to get space leaving the city.

When we got to the front of the long line of people waiting to leave town, the Southern Pacific official said, "We take refugees for free. Everybody else pays."

"Fine, we'll pay," said Uncle Thomas. "But we've got to get down to L.A."

"Refugees come first," said the trainman stubbornly. "Between the train and the ferries, we've already moved two hundred thousand folks out of the city. But the mayor wants all able-bodied men to stay to fight fires and help the injured—unless you're evacuating your family." He pointed at me. "Is he family?"

"Nephew. But we got to get to Los Angeles. I'm a re—"

"He looks big enough to help," the man interrupted. "Why don't you boys stay? You can help unload emergency supplies. Report right down there under that signal to Mr. O'Brian. He'll put you to work."

"We'd love to help," said Uncle Thomas impatiently, "but I'm a reporter for the *Los Angeles Daily Times*." He pulled his press card from his pocket. "The paper wants us back right away with our story."

The man stared at the card for several seconds through squinted eyes, then waved us on to board the train.

Travel out of the city was very slow, but once we reached the countryside, the speed picked up, and we didn't have the tiresome slowdowns we had experienced on the way north.

It was nearly evening when Uncle Thomas pulled out what was left of our bread and cheese and said, "Jerry, tell me more about what happened back there in Texas."

I squirmed in my seat. "Whadd'ya mean? I already told you about it."

"But why did this happen? What was actually going on?"

"I don' know. It was just an accident."

"But you're afraid if you go home, you'll be in big trouble—maybe even involving the sheriff. Is that it?"

"Yeah." I shrugged. "That's why Mama sent me

out to stay with you for a while—till it blows over." I looked out the window at the dry California landscape, painted in soft grays and purples in the fading light. Why was my uncle asking me all these questions?

"Jerry," he said, tapping my knee. I turned to see him looking sideways at me. "You think this is just goin' to blow over? If someone burned down your house, how long do you think it would take before you forgot about it?"

"I don't know. Pretty long, I guess."

"Now you're thinking straight. You know, it's not like they're goin' to pin it on someone else and let you off the hook. They're goin' to keep thinking about it, and when they know it wasn't Billy and Bob and—"

"It was Rod and JoJo and Clarence," I interrupted. I didn't like this conversation. It was like he was trying to be my dad or something.

"What?"

I rolled my head. "Those were the guys I was with. I don't know no Billy or Bob."

"Jerry, it doesn't matter who you were with. That's not the point! I'm trying to show you that this thing's not goin' to blow over just because you came out to California for a while. If no one else 'fesses up to it—and they won't—then it's going to remain unsolved but not forgotten. Someday you're goin' to have to deal with it."

I just kept looking out the window. He said no more about it, and neither did I. I already felt badly enough about that fire, so why did he have to keep bringing it up?

✧✧✧✧

It was late Saturday afternoon when we arrived back in Los Angeles. Joyous relatives and friends met some of the refugee families who had traveled all the way from San Francisco with us. Other refugees wandered into the station as wide-eyed and lost as if they had arrived in a foreign country.

A white man with a closely trimmed beard was scurrying from passenger to passenger handing out little pamphlets and saying, "If you've just come from San Francisco, this is of special importance to you."

I looked at the paper he had thrust into my hands. It was titled "The Earthquake: Did God Do That?" I started reading it as we walked through the depot.

"Hey, Uncle Thomas," I said. "This came from that Azusa Street Mission we visited last Tuesday. Listen to this: 'God does bring judgment on the earth when sin is too great.' An' it quotes some verses from the Bible." I read a couple. " 'When Thy judgments are in the earth, the inhabitants of the world learn righteousness.' It says that's from the book of Isaiah. And here: 'Thou shalt be visited of the Lord of Hosts with earthquakes, and great noise, and the flame of a devouring fire.' " I turned wide eyes to Uncle Thomas. "Wow! Sounds just like San Francisco to me!"

"Let me see that." Uncle Thomas took the pamphlet and scanned through it.

"You think that was a real prophecy we heard at

that church, Uncle Thomas?"

He shrugged. "What's a 'real' prophecy? The man said destruction was coming, and the next day it sure enough came, worst disaster this state has ever seen. Sounds like a true prophecy to me." He handed me back the paper as we got on the streetcar.

I felt a strange excitement. "Then maybe that speakin' in tongues and those healings were real, too. What do you think?"

He lifted both hands, palms up. "Hard to say. They could be just pullin' some old camp meetin' tricks. They pay some old coot a dollar to come hobblin' in on crutches and then throw them away as though he's been healed. And who knows what all that mumble jumble was?"

"But you said yourself that whites and blacks coming together was a miracle."

He nodded. "Indeed I did. Indeed I did." Suddenly he stood up. "I've got to get off here and go file my stories at the newspaper. You want to go on home? Think you can find your way?"

I nodded. I was tired and wanted to sleep someplace besides the ground or a train seat.

He moved toward the exit. "See you later. It might be late before I get home."

I rode the car to Alvarado Street. When I got off and started walking the short distance to my uncle's house, I couldn't help but remember the first time I had come up that street, just over two weeks before. So much had happened since. I really had been to the end of the earth and back, and now I felt older. But was I any wiser?

When I got to 142, a light was on inside. I warmed with the prospect of telling Lawrence about my adventures. Maybe Mrs. Catley would fix me a home-cooked meal, too. I was starved and tired of hard bread and cheese.

As I opened the door I called out, "Hello, I'm home!" so as not to startle Lawrence and Mrs. Catley.

Mrs. Catley came from the kitchen wiping her hands on a towel. "Lord have mercy, I'm glad to see you, Jerry Newman. I've been prayin' an' prayin' that both of you would be safe."

She was looking past me like she was expecting my uncle to follow me in the door. "Uncle Thomas stopped off at the newspaper. I think this was his big break. We took lots of pictures."

Then I was the one to look around. "Where's Lawrence? Didn't he come over with you this afternoon?"

"N-o-o." She drew the word out as she shook her head. "He's been doin' rather poorly the last few days. I've never seen him so discouraged, Jerry. Last night afore he went to sleep, he prayed, 'Lord, don't let me wake up.' It just broke my heart."

I felt a little guilty. The last couple days I'd been having the adventure of my life, not even thinking about Lawrence. But Lawrence . . . he was just stuck on a couch, sick, couldn't run around like other boys. Like me.

Chapter 10

Hope for Lawrence?

I WOKE TO SOMEONE SHAKING ME in the middle of the night. The light was on and I looked up sleepily into Uncle Thomas's grinning face.

"Guess what? They put me on full time. I'm a full-fledged staff reporter!" he announced. He was pacing back and forth in the little living room like a cat in a cage, waving his arms. "That earthquake was my big break! I go back in tomorrow afternoon. Have to work evenings and nights, but that's when a lot of news happens. I'll be the first one there to report it."

"That's great, Uncle Thomas," I mumbled. Then after a few groggy moments I asked, "Did the pictures come out?"

"Sure did, most of 'em, anyway. I might've been able to get you on as a photographer if you were older and didn't have to go back to school."

But when he finally snapped off the light and went into his room, I couldn't go back to sleep. *"School"*—did that mean Texas? Was he going to send me home now that he couldn't take me to work with him every day? There wasn't any need, far as I could see. I could take care of myself, go to school here in Los Angeles, maybe go over to the Catleys' some evenings.

In any case, I was not ready to go back to Romburg!

The next day, my uncle spent all day getting his clothes cleaned and ready for his new job. He even went out and bought a new pair of shoes. All that was just fine with me, because he didn't say a word about sending me back to Texas.

While he was bustling around, I went out and sat on the front step. I liked California. This is where I wanted to stay—especially when I thought about what faced me back in Texas. Then it struck me. If I wanted to stay, I'd better keep out of trouble. The quickest way for my uncle to send me home was to make trouble for him. He didn't need extra worries about me right now.

When afternoon came, I said, "Think I'll go over an' visit Lawrence this evening. Mrs. Catley said he's not doin' too well." Of course, I did want to see Lawrence, but I also didn't want my uncle worrying about me.

"Oh yeah, that sounds good," said Uncle Thomas. "Poor kid's probably as lonely as a raindrop in the Sahara. Tell him I hope he gets better." And that's all he said until it was time for him to leave for the newspaper.

"Gotta go now, Jerry. Think you can find yourself something to eat?"

"Yeah. I'll be fine. Bye, Uncle Thomas."

Whew! One more day in California!

When I got over to Lawrence's house, he was on his couch, wrapped in blankets and shivering from a chill. It didn't look like he'd been outside all day.

I told him all about the trip to San Francisco, and by the time I finished, his chill had passed. He propped himself up with pillows and told me how his mother lost two dozen quarts of canned tomatoes. "She had a bunch of wooden crates stacked up on the back porch to make shelves with jars of tomatoes sitting in them. The whole thing went over with that first quake. It made a crash like a train wreck."

Pretty soon we got out the checkers and were having a good game, but then Lawrence broke into a coughing fit. I stared. The stuff he spit up was all bloody. I went cold. Was Lawrence going to die? I couldn't imagine someone my age dying. Kids aren't supposed to die. Thinking about it made me feel really scared.

"One, two, three, Jerry," Lawrence said as he

jumped three of my men. He started to laugh at catching me daydreaming, but it kicked off another round of coughing that knocked him back on his pillow.

Guess I wasn't paying enough attention to our game. But I hadn't realized just how sick he was. Couldn't the doctors help him? If they couldn't, who could? The question no sooner passed through my mind than I thought: *God*. Could *God* heal him?

That preacher over on Azusa Street said God could heal. Would God help Lawrence if he went to that church on Azusa? That sure would be a test of whether or not they were fakes. I knew Lawrence was sick, seriously sick. If God healed him, that sure wouldn't be no "camp meetin' trick," as Uncle Thomas had called it.

I thought and thought on it while Lawrence whipped me at checkers, and then I said, "Hey, Lawrence. Think your mama would let you go out?"

"Guess so, if I felt up to it. Why?"

How would I explain this? "Well, I went to this unusual church with my uncle. There're people there who've been healed of all kinds of things. In fact, a woman was healed of tuberculosis—just like you got—the very night we visited." I stopped, trying to think how to put it. "Anyway, been thinkin' they might be able to help you, too. A little prayer couldn't hurt anybody, right?"

"Mama prays for me every night and day." Lawrence looked down and then mumbled, "So far hasn't done any good."

"But this place is really different," I said. "They say they got the Holy Ghost, and they speak in different languages, and everything. Uncle Thomas and I went upstairs, and there were crutches and braces and eyeglasses and every sort of thing from people who didn't need 'em anymore. They'd been healed. It might work for you, too. Whadd'ya say?"

"Go to a church? Tonight? Aw, I don't know." He shook his head. "My mom couldn't go. She's workin' at the Auditorium Hotel tonight. My papa's already working in the hotel kitchen, and Mama's goin' to serve at some big banquet or something. They always tryin' to earn extra money, what with my doctor bills and all."

Lawrence started to set up the checkerboard for another game. "Gotta admit, it sure would be fun to go out. Gets pretty boring round here, especially when I'm alone. Say, Jerry, can you stay this evening?"

"Sure. My uncle works tonight."

I tried to concentrate on the game. We had exchanged two moves each, when he asked casually, "How far away is that church?"

"Just downtown."

A grin spread across his face. We were getting the same idea at the same time, but I said it first. "We could take the streetcar. It's just a block and a half off First Street."

"That's not near so far as walking from here over to your house with Mama."

"Think you could do it?"

He shrugged. “At least you’d be there if I needed someone to lean on.”

We made it to the mission, stopping every once in a while to let Lawrence rest—he seemed so much weaker. The service was already in progress when we arrived, and the crowd was again overflowing the box-shaped building. However, people could tell by looking at Lawrence that he was sick, and they kindly stepped aside to let us in.

“Follow me,” said a tall man in a gray suit when we entered. He was partially bald, and the little blond hair he had was slicked back, making his head as smooth as a bullet. He put a chair near the front for Lawrence, but I had to stand to one side.

Pastor Seymour was already preaching. I looked around the room to see whether I recognized any of the people who had been there on my first visit—possibly the old Indian who had prayed for the white woman. But I couldn’t pick him out in the crowd.

Finally William Seymour’s words caught my attention. “Why are you here tonight?” he asked. “Did you just come to see some kind of a Holy Ghost show? Or have you come in faith? Why have you come?”

He launched into a story. “When I was a boy, I was returning home one night after dark and took a shortcut through a cemetery, thinking I was mighty brave for doing so. I was marching along, determined not to run, when suddenly I saw ahead of me

what looked like a figure of a man without his head. I froze, fighting fear and the urge to flee. 'It's just some strangely shaped gravestone,' I told myself. Then suddenly it began to move, walking slowly right toward me. Still, I held my ground, blinking and hoping my eyes were just playing tricks on me. Then I heard the specter's feet crunching on dry grass and twigs, and I knew I was facing more than just shadows.

"When the phantom was no more than a few yards away, it raised its head . . . and I saw with great relief that it was not a man but an old horse that had simply been grazing its way through the cemetery with its head to the ground."

A titter rippled through the congregation, who'd been hanging on his words.

Seymour fixed us with his good eye. "So what do you expect to see here tonight? Some people jumping around all happy? People speaking in tongues?"

I looked over at Lawrence. I knew what I wanted to see. I wanted to see him get help. But would that happen?

Pastor Seymour continued, "If you came seeking tongues, you are on a wrong search. Do not seek to speak with tongues. Seek the promise of the Father, and pray for the baptism with the Holy Ghost.

"The Scripture says, 'When the day of Pentecost was fully come, they were all with one accord in one place. And suddenly there came a sound from heaven as of a rushing mighty wind, and it filled all the house where they were sitting. And there appeared unto them cloven tongues like as of fire, and it sat upon each of them. And they were all filled with the Holy Ghost, and began to speak with other tongues, as the Spirit gave them utterance.' "

At the mention of tongues of fire, I began to feel just as uncomfortable as if *I* had seen a headless man walking in a cemetery. This was the same Bible passage the preacher in Romburg was speaking from when we boys had decided to play a trick with our cattail torches.

"Now, beloved," Pastor Seymour said, "do not be too concerned about speaking in tongues. Let the Holy Ghost give you utterance, and it will come just as freely as the air we breathe. It is nothing to be worked up. It comes from the heart. You see, God has a purpose for the gift of tongues. On the day of Pentecost, people from all over the world were in Jerusalem—just like we have people from many races here with us tonight.

"The gift of tongues enabled everyone to hear the Gospel, as has happened here among us. Our unity, the fact that people from every race receive the Gospel and are welcomed into one body, is the proof that the Father has poured out His Holy Ghost on us."

I looked around the room. The place was packed—probably over a thousand people inside and out. The majority were black, but there were also many whites and Mexicans, some Asians and people with turbans, possibly from India or the Middle East.

"Think about it!" said Pastor Seymour. "Every year hundreds of black people are lynched by white people in this country. But here in this place, we gather in love as the color line disappears and a new type of Christian community is born."

I knew about lynchings. JoJo's cousin said something some white man didn't like, and they found him swinging from a tree. That was the reason blacks in Romburg pretty much stayed to themselves.

Like Uncle Thomas said, this racial mixing was nothing short of a miracle.

"Now let me ask you another question," said Pastor Seymour. "What are *you* afraid of here tonight? Are you ready to receive the Holy Ghost? You know you can't play with the Holy Ghost. You can't mock Him. Don't forget what happened to Ananias and Sapphira."

Pastor Seymour stopped preaching and lifted his hands and closed his eyes in prayer. But his quiet words did not sound like English, and I realized that he was praying in tongues. My mind drifted back to what he had just said. Who were Ananias and Sapphira? I knew I'd heard of their names before . . . and then it came to me. They were the husband and wife in the Bible who'd fallen down dead after telling a lie about giving all their money to the church, when they'd actually kept part of it back. The apostle Peter had said they'd lied to the Holy Ghost. Mocking the Holy Ghost was dangerous business.

Goosebumps crawled up my spine, like I'd just come out of warm water into a cold breeze. I hung my head, staring at the floor. Had I mocked the Holy Ghost by pretending to be His tongues of fire outside that church in Texas? Is that why my little joke had turned into such a disaster? But then . . . I hadn't fallen down dead. It was the church that had burned down. The church had received the worst of it . . . or had I? Here I was, over a thousand miles from Romburg, and unable to return home.

"Son . . . you there, young man . . . would you step

forward to the altar?"

I snapped my head up. Was Pastor Seymour speaking to me? Had he somehow seen into my heart and discovered the terrible deed I'd done? But he was not speaking to me. He was talking to Lawrence.

Lawrence stood up shakily, coughed once, and stepped forward.

"The Lord has a special blessing for you, son," said the preacher. "Are you willing to receive it?"

Lawrence nodded, his eyes wide.

Pastor Seymour came around the makeshift pulpit, reached out and placed his hands on either side of Lawrence's head, and continued praying in tongues. Then with a shout, his hands flew out from Lawrence's head: "In the name of Jesus, be healed." He then placed his right hand on the center of Lawrence's chest and quietly said, "There, that's it. Receive it!"

At first I thought he had hit Lawrence or given a big push, because Lawrence fell straight back. But he hadn't hit him or pushed him. Lawrence just fell like a tree chopped down in the woods.

The same man who had gotten a chair for Lawrence when we came in was right behind Lawrence and caught him. Otherwise, I'm sure Lawrence would have crashed to the floor. The man gently laid Lawrence down on the floor, and I thought my sick friend had died right before my eyes.

Oh no, oh, God, my sins—my mockery of the Holy Ghost—had caught up to me. But it was not I who had died, but poor, innocent Lawrence.

"No!" I screamed, but my cry was drowned out as the crowd began to sing.

"The Comforter has come,
    The Comforter has come!
The Holy Ghost from Heaven,
    The Father's promise given;
O spread the tidings 'round,
    wherever man is found—
The Comforter has come!"

Chapter 11

Walking and Leaping and Praising God

I LEAPED FORWARD, but the man with the thin, blond hair caught me and held me back. "It's all right, son," he spoke into my ear. "Your friend's fine. He's just restin' in the Lord."

"What do you mean, restin'? He's not even breathin'!"

"Oh yes, he is."

"But you gotta help him. He's got tuberculosis. He might die!" I struggled to break free, but the man held me firmly as the people continued to sing.

"Just calm down, son. He's under the care of the best Physician in the universe. Hold on, son. The devils may be howling and the hypocrites a-growling, but the Christians are shouting, and the Holy Ghost is workin' on him. So just stand back. Hallelujah!"

His words more than his grip held me back. Where I came from, white people didn't talk like that. If this was the Holy Ghost's work, I knew I'd better not interfere. I didn't want to be in danger of mocking Him again. But, boy, was it hard to stay put. I felt like I was the one walking through that cemetery Pastor Seymour told about, and I was terrified of what I'd seen. But Lawrence was breathing. I could now see that clearly, so I held steady.

"The Comforter has come," the people sang. . . .

"The Comforter has come!
The Holy Ghost from Heaven,
The Father's promise given . . ."

Lawrence began to move, and then he opened his eyes and stared, openmouthed, toward the ceiling as though there were some great painting displayed there. His gaze was so intense that I glanced up myself, but all I saw were plain, old whitewashed boards.

Then he tried to get up. This time the man released me as I lunged to help my friend. "Are you okay?" I asked, but he didn't answer. He just kept gazing up as he struggled to his feet.

When he was standing and still clinging to my arm, he finally broke his gaze from the ceiling and looked around at the people who were still singing and swaying to the easy swing of the old Holy Ghost hymn. Suddenly he began to smile and breathe in deep breaths, each one larger than the previous one.

Then it struck me that such deep breathing wasn't making him cough!

His breaths out became laughs, and still he didn't cough. His grin got wider and he looked me in the eye. "I can breathe again, Jerry! I can breathe!"

He even tried to cough, but it didn't catch. There was no hacking. Nothing rattled in his chest, and nothing doubled him over with the pain and desperation I had so often seen.

"Hey!" he yelled above the people's singing, waving his arms in the air to get their attention. "Hey, everybody! Hey!"

The singing tapered off until just a few around the edges and outside the door were carrying the tune, and then one lone voice stopped as though someone had pinched it off.

"Hey, everybody, I . . . I think I've been . . ." Lawrence took two huge breaths, so deep that he leaned back with each one in order to draw in more air. "Yeah, I've . . . I've been healed!" He jumped as though he were trying to see the last person at the back of the crowd, and this time he yelled, "I've been healed! I've been healed! I've been healed!"

He kept jumping higher and higher, as if he had springs under his feet.

"Lawrence. Lawrence!" I waved my hands, trying to calm him down. "Lawrence, you gotta calm down." By then, even I would've been exhausted from jumping around, but he paid no attention.

Suddenly a thin, old woman with watery eyes, who stood near the front of the circle that surrounded the makeshift altar, held a tambourine high and began beating it against the heel of her left hand. Once she got a driving rhythm going, she shouted, "Glory!" and began to sing. Everyone quickly joined in.

"When I think about Jesus
And what He's done for me,
When I think about Jesus
And how He's set me free,
I could dance, dance, dance, dance,
Da-a-a-ance, all night!"

They repeated the song, and repeated it again and again, faster and faster, as people at first clapped in time and tapped their feet. But soon the foot tapping became a light-footed shuffle that broke into a full dance with arms swinging and feet skipping faster than beads of water on a hot skillet.

"Go on!" yelled the white man with the slicked-back hair to Lawrence. "It's the Holy Ghost dance. You can do it!"

"Oh no," I said, reaching out to grab Lawrence's arm, but he elbowed me away and began bobbing in time with the music.

I looked down at his feet and saw that he had picked up the double-timing step with each foot. "Come on, Jerry. It's the Holy Ghost dance! God has healed me!"

I didn't know what to do. I felt as out of place as a

cactus in a cattle stampede, so I began timidly clapping my hands in time with the music and swaying my head from side to side just a little bit so I wouldn't look too different.

The dancing and singing went on for a good ten minutes until, one after another, people collapsed in their chairs from sheer exhaustion. But even though sweat rolled off Lawrence's grinning face, he didn't slow down the whole time.

Two or three times Pastor Seymour tried to bring the celebration to a halt. But he no sooner slowed the "fire" to a warm glow than it would break forth in a new round of enthusiasm, and he would throw up his hands with a smile and join in for a little more singing and dancing himself.

When finally the people had quieted, he said simply, "God is so good, isn't He?"

It was like touching a spark to a keg of gunpowder. The hallelujahs and glories and clapping broke forth again with new joy.

"There're people who came here tonight to criticize and mock," he said above the simmering din, "but if you stay, you'll end up on your knees down here at the altar asking the Lord's forgiveness and seeking the blessing for yourself."

He remained quiet for a few minutes while the whole crowd slowly calmed down. I could hear some quiet sobbing from different points in the room. At first I wondered why people would be crying, but then I remembered there were such things as tears of joy. Maybe that was why people were crying.

Pastor Seymour said, "The reason why there are so many of God's people without divine power today, without experiential salvation worked out in their hearts by the blood, by the power of the blessed Holy Spirit, is because they have not accepted Him as their Teacher, as their Leader, as their Comforter. Jesus said in His precious Word that if He went away, He would send us another Comforter. The need of men and women today is for a Comforter. And praise our God! We have received this blessed Comforter, and it is heaven in our souls. We can sing with all our hearts . . ." And he burst out in song:

> "What matter where on earth we dwell
> On mountain top, or in the dell,
> In cottage or a mansion fair,
> Where Jesus is, 'tis heaven there."

Without missing a beat he went on. "In John 14, Jesus said, 'Greater works than these shall [you] do; because I go unto my Father, . . . and he shall give you another Comforter, that he may abide with you for ever.' The 'works' Jesus spoke of were His miracles, but the miracles most Christians do certainly aren't *greater*. In fact, they're not even a shadow of what Jesus did. They don't heal people. They don't live holy lives. They don't prophesy in God's name. Some preachers even argue that Holy Ghost signs ended long ago even though Jesus promised the Comforter would abide with us forever. Why? Why do they say these things?

"Could it be that they never asked, so didn't receive; didn't seek, so couldn't find; failed to knock, so no door opened, and so now they have to explain why their works aren't greater? Jesus said, 'Wait for the promise of the Father, [and] ye shall be baptized with the Holy Ghost.' He said, 'Tarry . . . until ye be endued with power from on high.' But some people are too impatient to wait, too proud to get down and tarry, seeking His holy promise with their whole hearts.

"But bless His holy name! May God help every one of His blood-bought children to receive this blessed Comforter. Glory to His name! Hallelujah! Hosanna to His omnipotent name! Oh, He is reigning in my soul tonight! Hallelujah!"

The preaching was over, and I was exhausted as we emerged from the Azusa Street Mission and walked to the corner where we could catch a streetcar.

"I'm well, Jerry! I'm well," Lawrence said, slapping me on the back. "Wait until my mom and dad see me. Hey, let's forget the streetcar and walk home. I haven't had a good walk for a long time."

"Lawrence, you gotta calm down. I'm glad you're feeling better, but you should be sensible. This damp night air isn't good for someone in your condition."

"My condition? What's wrong with my condition? Come on!"

We started walking, me watching him to be sure he didn't start staggering or coughing. "You really think you're . . . healed?"

"Couldn't feel better!" He laughed.

"What did it feel like?"

"What did *what* feel like?"

"You know, when you were down there on the

floor—man, I thought you were dead."

He shook his head. "I sure wasn't dead, but it did seem like I was in some other place, not really away, just quiet and peaceful. I kind of knew people were around, but not really."

"But what about your tuberculosis? What happened to it?"

Lawrence patted his chest softly with his left hand and shrugged. "I don't know. When I was down on the floor, there seemed to be kind of a warm tingling in my chest, but even that wasn't very strong . . . just a faint warmth." He turned and grinned at me. "Maybe that was God healing me. Did you see anything?"

"All I saw was Pastor Seymour hit you in the chest with his hand."

"He didn't hit me. He didn't even push me."

"Then why did you fall down?"

"I don't know. Suddenly I just couldn't stand up anymore."

We walked on for a block or so in silence, me thinking back over everything that had happened that evening. Finally I asked, "Do you *really* think you've been healed?"

"Yeah, no question!"

"When did you know it? I mean, when did you know you were well?"

Lawrence didn't answer immediately. I looked at him but couldn't read his expression in the dark. When he spoke, his voice had a faraway sound. "I felt good when I woke up—I mean, I wasn't really asleep.

But anyway, when I stood up, I didn't cough. I think that's when I knew something was different, so I tried taking a breath, and I still didn't cough."

He didn't explain anything more, and I didn't ask any more questions. I guess I was starting to believe that the Holy Ghost might have actually healed Lawrence, and that made me a little scared. I was still curious about other details, but I began to feel like I was intruding on something private, maybe even holy.

By the time we got to Lawrence's house it was late, and even though his parents weren't there, I decided to go on home. I didn't want Uncle Thomas to start worrying about me if he got home first.

The next day just after noon, Lawrence came banging on our front door. I was afraid he would wake up Uncle Thomas, who was still sleeping in, but apparently he was awake because he called out for me to see who was at the door.

Lawrence came bounding in like a frisky puppy. "Guess what! Mama took me to the doctor this morning, and he *agrees* that I'm cured! Says there's still evidence that I used to have tuberculosis, but the sickness is gone." He grinned widely. "Doc wants to keep watching me, but for now, I can go anywhere I want."

"Does he think God healed you?" I asked. Why did I still feel so amazed?

"God healed who?" asked Uncle Thomas, coming into the living room, buttoning up his shirt.

"Me!" announced Lawrence, holding his arms out to his sides as though he were presenting himself for inspection.

My uncle raised a critical eyebrow. "Well, you sure do look better. Glad to see it. Last I heard you were going downhill."

"Not anymore." Lawrence's grin got even bigger. "Last night we went to that Azusa Street Mission. Pastor Seymour prayed for me, and God healed me!"

"He *what*?" Uncle Thomas turned to me, a frown on his face. "Jerry, did you go down there last night without asking me?" he challenged.

Uh-oh. My heart sank. It looked like I was in trouble again. But . . . how could I be in trouble after such a good thing came of our little trip the night before?

Chapter 12

Facing the Music

I WAS ONLY TRYIN' TO HELP LAWRENCE!" I said to my uncle. "And see? He's actually better. I mean, look at him. He's all well."

Uncle Thomas scowled at me, then shifted his gaze to Lawrence. "Come here, son, and turn around."

When Lawrence obeyed, my uncle put his ear to my friend's back. "Now breathe real deep," he ordered. "Again . . . and again." Like he was a doctor himself.

" 'Member what you said 'bout camp meetin' tricks—"

"Hush, Jerry. I'm tryin' to listen to his lungs, and I can't hear anything if you keep blabbin'."

A few deep breaths later, my

uncle raised his head. “Can’t hear a thing,” he said, glaring at me again.

“Like I said, ’member what you said ’bout camp meetin’ tricks? Well, for sure this ain’t no trick, ’cause Lawrence was sure enough sick—powerful sick. We knew it, everybody knew it, even the doctor, but now he’s well. So . . . so doesn’t that prove it?” I paused, not sure where I was going with my comments. I just didn’t want my uncle to think I’d been causing trouble by going down to the Azusa Mission without asking. Without waiting for his answer, I rushed on. “Just think about it, Uncle Thomas. You said yourself it was a miracle for blacks and whites to get together like that . . . an’ then—an’ then there was the prophecy about the earthquake. It came true! And now we know Lawrence really got healed. So . . . what do you think?”

“Think about what?”

I couldn’t read his face. “About . . . about whether we’ve discovered a for-real Holy Ghost . . . Pentecostal church . . . or whatever.” I ended my “presentation” with my arms out like I had just revealed a pot of gold.

My uncle glared at me. “So what? Right now I’m not interested in miracles or some new church or anything but you.”

“But . . . but . . .” I swallowed hard, my throat tightening like I was wringing out a washrag.

“Listen, Jerry. I don’t mind that you went to that church, and I’m certainly glad that Lawrence is better—” he glanced toward Lawrence—“that he . . . got healed, or whatever you want to call it. But you've got to grow up, and that means behavin' in a responsible manner. I've got a full-time job now. I can't be watching out for you every minute, and it would take a book if I tried to list all the things you should and shouldn't do. I can't do that. You've got to be responsible yourself." He pointed at Lawrence. "This kid could have died on you. Did you ever think of that?"

It had crossed my mind, but I hadn't really considered it. I shook my head miserably.

Uncle Thomas turned to Lawrence. "Weren't your folks upset that you went out last night without them knowing?"

"No, sir. Guess they were so glad I was healed, they didn't think about what might have happened."

"Well, I'm glad for you, too. But, Jerry," he said, turning back to me, "you gotta use your head. Remember when you told me about that trouble back in Romburg? It didn't happen because you were *trying* to be bad. It happened because you didn't *think* about the possible consequences."

He stopped, and I looked down at the floor to avoid his gaze. Somehow his assurance that he didn't think of me as a bad person brought tears to my eyes. At least Uncle Thomas understood that I hadn't meant to do any harm. But in exchange for that relief came a proper burden: I had been living irresponsibly. Too often I didn't think before I acted. Now, *that* was true, and I knew it.

"Jerry," said my uncle, "wanna know what I think? It's time you went back to Texas and faced the music. What do *you* think?"

I nodded slowly. I took some comfort knowing he wasn't trying to get rid of me. But he was right. I couldn't keep running from that fire. Facing my responsibility was part of growing up, part of becoming a man. Something I had to do.

I didn't exactly know why, but there was something I wanted to do first. "Could I go back to the Azusa Street Mission once more—'fore I go back to Texas?"

"Suit yourself."

I glanced at Lawrence. "All right if Lawrence comes with me?"

My uncle shrugged. "Okay by me—but *this* time you boys ask his mama."

Lawrence wasn't able to go with me. We went right over to his house to ask, but his mother had already invited some friends over to celebrate "Lawrence's miracle."

Since there wasn't anything else for me to do, I went on down to the mission as soon as my uncle left for work. I arrived early, long before the service was to start. When I stepped into the square little building, two or three people were cleaning up and rearranging the benches and chairs.

I stood there, not knowing whether to help or wander out for a walk until the service started.

"Afternoon, son."

I whirled around. Pastor Seymour had come in behind me. I grabbed my hat off my head and nodded to him, somehow lost for words at the moment.

"Weren't you here last night with that young boy who was so sick?"

"Yes, sir." I bobbed my head. "That was Lawrence Catley. He couldn't come tonight, but I reckon he'll be back soon enough."

"And how is he?"

"Fine! He's just fine." I bit my lip, feeling a little awkward talking to such a man of God. "His mother took him to the doctor this mornin', and he said his tuberculosis is all cleared up."

"Tuberculosis, was it. Well, praise the name of Jesus."

I found it hard to know which eye to look at when talking with Pastor Seymour. I didn't want to stare at his sightless eye, but then it felt strange to focus only on the other one. I guess you usually look back and forth between a person's eyes.

"And what about you?" he interrupted my eye gazing.

"M-me? I'm doin' pretty good, sir."

"Just 'pretty good'?"

I rolled my hat in my hands. Out through the open door I noticed the afternoon breeze kick up a small swirl of dust in the street. Somehow I sensed that if I brushed off the pastor with just some pleasant response, he would know it wasn't the whole story. I looked down at my shoes. "Pretty good for havin' to go back to Texas tomorrow."

"Texas, huh. You know, I lived in Houston for quite a while. What part of Texas are you from?"

"Romburg. A little town north—"

"Of course. I know where Romburg is, not fifty miles northeast of Houston. I preached up there one Sunday at . . . at—what was his name?—Mason, Rev. Mason. Yeah, I preached up there at his church. Nice little town, right there along the Trinity River. . . . What's wrong, son? You don't look so good." Seymour reached out and put his hand on my shoulder for a moment.

I don't know what came over me, but suddenly I was spilling out the whole story to Pastor Seymour—practically a total stranger—about me burning that church.

When I had finished, he just stood there nodding his head and saying, "Hmmm . . . hmmm," while rubbing his hands together kind of slow like he was washing them. Finally he sucked in a deep breath. "So now you've got to go back, is that it?"

I nodded miserably. "Yes, sir. My uncle says I've got to face the music and take responsibility, but—" I stopped because I didn't know what else to say. Part of me wanted to do what was right, but most of me wanted to run.

"Tell me, son, have you ever taken this problem to the Lord?"

"Oh yes. I prayed several times that somehow God would turn back the clock and make it not so. I even went down to that pine grove just hoping He had answered my prayer and that the church would still be standing there. But I guess He didn't hear me."

A smile played on the pastor's mouth. "Oh, I reckon He heard you. But that's not usually the way God works. I can think of only one time in the Bible where God turned back the clock, but that wasn't to reverse evil, it was just to give King Hezekiah a sign."

"Then what can I do?" I put my hand over my eyes like a sunshade so he wouldn't see the tears that I couldn't hold back.

"Do you know about repentance and forgiveness?"

I shrugged. I'd said I was sorry for getting in trouble more times than I could count—Mama always made me. But I didn't know what good it did. I was usually still in as much trouble after I said it as before.

"Come on upstairs with me," said Pastor Seymour, putting his arm around my shoulder. "I think I've got some good news for you about Jesus' blood."

I cringed at his mention of blood, but I went with him anyway.

It was nearly sundown four days later when I stepped off the train in Romburg. Mama didn't even know I was coming home, so no one was waiting for me. I adjusted my cap and slipped on the light jacket that Uncle Thomas had given to me as a going-home gift. *"Tell your mother this is in payment for all the hard work you did in San Francisco,"* he had said. *"You know, Jerry, I really appreciate your help. I*

couldn't have done it without you. And now I have a real reporter's job."

After a hoot from its whistle, the train chugged slowly out of the station, spewing steam with every puff. I felt like a ghost as I stepped off the platform, crossed the tracks, and headed toward home. So much had happened to me, but the town looked the same, and no one seemed to notice me.

I wasn't far from home when I heard singing floating over the still evening air. I listened and changed my direction to follow the sound. It was coming from the edge of town, down toward the river. I followed it and finally realized that it came from the old pine grove where the A.M.E. Church had stood.

For a moment my heart caught. Maybe God had done a miracle after all and turned back the clock. Maybe the little white church would still be standing there. Maybe all my troubles would be over.

The cattails in the ditch had gone to seed, and fluffy cotton was spewing from each head. I didn't pick any as I took a shortcut across the ditch and through the trees. Up ahead I could see lights, and as I got closer, the singing became clearer. And then I was at the edge of the clearing.

In front of the site of the old church, there now stood a large tent with two peaks and the sides rolled up. From the posts around the edge hung lanterns, and inside benches had been arranged for about forty people who were standing and clapping and swaying to the slow, passionate rhythm.

"I will trust in the Lord,
    I will trust in the Lord.
I will trust in the Lord,
    till I die."

I smiled at the old spiritual. It was one I actually remembered from when Mama took me to church as a child. I walked slowly to where I could see more clearly, just outside the circle of light. Unconsciously, I started to sing along until I realized they were making up new words.

"Fo' our chuch dats been burn' down,
    Fo' our chuch dats been burn' down,
Fo' our chuch dats been burn' down,
    Thank You, Lord."

What? They were thanking the Lord even though their church was gone? I wasn't sure I'd heard right.

Suddenly I realized that Rev. Mason had noticed me and was straining to see who I was. Not knowing whether I should leave or stay, I pulled off my cap, and then he motioned with his finger for me to enter.

This wasn't the way I had planned it. I was going to have a private conversation with Rev. Mason, and . . . but now it seemed too late. Walking cautiously as though I might wake someone from a light sleep, I slipped into the back of the tent and found a seat on the end of one of the benches.

After the song the people sat down, and then the pastor had a straight view of me.

"Young man, we're glad you're here. Do you have something to say to us tonight?"

Everyone turned around and looked at me with such silent expectation that I found myself standing to my feet, spinning my hat in my hands.

"Well, I . . . I just arrived from California, and I . . ."

I had been about to tell them that I was there to bring them greetings from Pastor Seymour and the

Azusa Street Mission. He'd told me that I should bring his greetings, but that was not really why I was there.

"I . . . I guess . . . I—" The words I'd planned to say escaped me. So I gave up and just blurted out, "Rev. Mason, I was the one who burned down your church. I didn't mean to. I was just pretending to hold 'tongues of fire' up by your windows. But I tripped, an' my cattail torch fell into the old Christmas tree, and . . ." I shrugged, indicating that after that, it was all over.

The people were just staring at me. "If you were in California, why have you come back, son?" said the pastor. His face was tipped slightly up as though he were looking at me through the bottoms of eyeglasses, even though he didn't wear any.

I swallowed. "I . . . I'm here to say I'm sorry an' to ask your forgiveness. In Los Angeles, at the Azusa Street Mission, I asked God to forgive me. And I know He forgave me and saved me, but . . . but Pastor Seymour said the first miracle in my life needed to be the courage to face you all. He said the Holy Ghost would give me the strength, an' . . . an' I guess He has, 'cause here I am."

I looked around. All the people who had turned in their seats were still staring at me as though they thought I would disappear if they blinked.

"Don' know what I can do," I continued, "but right here and now I'm committing myself to help rebuild this church. I'll work till I get it paid off, however long it takes."

Still they stared.

"And when I'm done, maybe . . . maybe I can worship with you, if you'll have me."

Rev. Mason cleared his throat loudly. "I don't believe that's acceptable, young man."

My heart sank. They weren't going to forgive me!

He paused and scratched the back of his head. "I think I speak for the rest of this here congregation when I say we most certainly do forgive you, but . . . the doors of this church are open to you *right now*, if you will." He laughed. "We not gonna wait till we have some actual doors on a building. You part of us right now!"

I looked around, a little confused. But the people on the benches were nodding and saying, "That right. . . . C'mon, now."

"Come on up here," Rev. Mason said, his voice so husky that he had to clear his throat again. "Everybody, let's pray for this young man—Mr. Gerald Fredrick Newman, isn't that right?"

"Yes, sir."

I moved forward, looking from side to side at the people who were smiling and nodding at me as they got up from their benches to follow me down to the altar. Then it crossed my mind in the middle of that intense situation: How did Rev. Mason know my first, last, and middle names?

His prayer was brief, thanking God for saving me and bringing me back to Romburg and to their little congregation. Then he asked God to bless me. I never thought I'd be so glad to be back from the end of the earth and in that dusty little east Texas town as I was right then.

When he finished praying, he said, "Now, this Pastor Seymour, would that be William J. Seymour?" As I nodded, he reached behind his makeshift pulpit and pulled out a small newspaper. "I think we have been reading something he's written." He looked at the top of the page and read, " '*The Apostolic Faith*, volume one, number one, from Los Angeles, California.' Were you out there, son, at this mission on 312 Azusa Street?"

I nodded again. He continued to read. "It says here, 'Pentecost has surely come and with it the Bible evidences are following, many being converted and sanctified and filled with the Holy Ghost, speaking in tongues as they did on the day of Pentecost.' Is that true? Are these things happening?"

When I confirmed that, yes, those things seemed to be happening, he started peppering me with questions. I answered as best I could, telling him about Lawrence and the tongues sometimes being interpreted from languages people understood. Then I told him about the different races all coming together in one place. "Pastor Seymour says that only God's love can unite blacks and whites, Indian and Chinese and South American," I explained. "He said the blood of Jesus washed away the color line."

There was silence for several moments after I said that, and I began to wonder if I had said something wrong. Finally Rev. Mason said, "Is this actually happening?"

I lit up. "Oh yes, sir. There's blacks and whites and everybody there! My uncle said he's never seen anything like it."

Rev. Mason shook his head in wonder, then turned his face up and raised his hands. "Then, O Lord, let your Holy Ghost fall on us *tonight*, right here in east Texas, right now." He then looked around at the people who had come forward to pray for me. "If any of you wish to go home, feel free to be dismissed. But the rest of us are going to kneel down here and pray on through. We'll tarry the whole night if need be, but it's time to ask God to baptize us with His Holy Ghost and fire. This is it!"

He and most of the people found a bench to kneel at and began to pray.

Almost without realizing it, I dropped to my knees in the middle of them.

More About William Seymour

TODAY, THE SPIRITUAL HEIRS of the Azusa Street Revival number over half a billion, making Pentecostals and charismatics the second largest and the fastest-growing family of Christians in the world. Whether black or white, Hispanic or Asian, almost all churches in this movement can trace their roots directly or indirectly to the humble mission at 312 Azusa Street and its pastor, William J. Seymour.

Seymour was born on May 2, 1870, in Centerville, Louisiana, to Simon and Phyllis Seymour, former slaves, who raised him as a Baptist. In his youth, William often had visions of God and studied the Scriptures diligently. At the age of twenty-five, he moved to Indianapolis, where he worked as a railroad porter and a waiter in a fashionable restaurant.

His church while in Indianapolis was a black Methodist Episcopal Church.

In 1900 he moved to Cincinnati, Ohio, and enrolled in a Holiness Bible School that emphasized sanctification (being made holy), divine healing, and the expectation that there would be a worldwide Holy Spirit revival before the Lord's soon return. Seymour heard God call him to become a preacher, but he resisted until he caught smallpox, a disease that often killed its victims, and left poor William blind in his left eye. After he recovered, he felt his illness had been a punishment for not obeying God's call. So he immediately accepted ordination as a preacher.

He then moved to Houston, Texas, to find and then live with some relatives lost during slavery. From 1903 to 1905 he accepted several short-term preaching assignments. He also met a black woman, Mrs. Lucy Farrow, who claimed to have spoken in unknown tongues while accompanying evangelist Charles F. Parham and his family to Kansas as their governess. Earlier in Topeka, a woman named Agness Ozman had spoken in unknown tongues, and Parham considered this the first evidence of a Pentecost-like renewal. He had not yet experienced it himself, but he preached that it was coming. Now that the Parhams and Mrs. Farrow had returned to Houston, Seymour wanted to learn more. Parham, however, was a determined segregationist, and he would not allow Seymour to sit in his classroom with white students. So Seymour arranged to sit in the hallway outside the open door and listen to Parham's lectures. Theologically they made sense to Seymour, though he could not abide Parham's racism.

One day William Seymour received a letter from a small church in Los Angeles. One of its members had heard Seymour preach when she had visited relatives in Houston. The church invited him to be their pastor, and they had included a train ticket in the letter.

Seymour arrived and preached his Pentecostal message in a house church until after a month of intense prayer and fasting, the Holy Spirit fell in power on the small group and several spoke in tongues in April 1906. The experience was like fire, in that word spread so quickly that the crowds who came broke the porch on the little house, and the group had to look for another building. They found and rented a former church—then used as a warehouse—at 312 Azusa Street. Meetings were held daily and late into each night for the next three years, often six hundred people at a time crowded into the little church with five or six hundred more outside listening through the windows.

Initially the secular press and the religious leaders who opposed this movement pointed to the more dramatic spiritual gifts—the healing, prophecy, and speaking in tongues—as characteristics either to mock or question. But those were not the qualities that William Seymour believed were the most important demonstrations of the Holy Spirit's baptism and not the ones he emphasized in his teaching. "Tongues are one of the signs that go with every baptized person, but it is not the real evidence of the baptism in the everyday life," he wrote.[1]

Seymour believed that the real miracle on the Day of Pentecost as recorded in Acts 2 was the Holy Spirit's outpouring of so much godly love that three thousand people from "every nation under heaven" accepted the Gospel in one day. The unity Jesus prayed for in John 17 was dramatically realized between former enemies and strangers. The gift of tongues was merely a means of communicating that love. And so for Seymour, love that could unite blacks and whites, people from India and China and South America, was what mattered. He said that if people weren't expressing this 1 Corinthians 13 kind of love, then "I care not how many tongues you may have, you have not the baptism with the Holy Spirit."[2] As far as Seymour was concerned, the blood of Jesus washed away the color line in Christ's church.

Black people—many only a generation removed from slavery and terrified by the thousands of lynchings still occurring to their race—embraced white brothers and sisters in the Lord at Azusa. Sophisticated white people humbled themselves and asked black people to "actually" lay hands on them and pray for them. This mixing among the races mesmerized and alarmed the world. But the new "Pentecostals," as they were by then called, rose up from their knees praising God, healed of their fear and hatred, and volunteered to go to other cities or foreign countries as missionaries. Many were confident that the tongues the Holy Spirit enabled them to speak equipped them to communicate with non-

English-speaking people. Indeed, while these Pentecostals most often spoke in a heavenly prayer and praise language, dozens of reports confirmed that sometimes messages in recognized foreign languages came from people who previously knew only English.

Within two years, the movement took root in over fifty nations around the world. Seymour's newspaper, *The Apostolic Faith*, reached a circulation of fifty thousand. Unquestionably, something real was happening.

But jealousy and strife also took root.

Not all white people liked the idea of a humble black man with such a significant ministry. In late October 1906, evangelist Charles F. Parham, the Texan who had allowed Seymour to sit outside of his classroom of white students, came to Los Angeles. Seymour received him respectfully, but it was soon apparent that Parham intended to take over the Azusa Street Mission. In his first message, he declared, "God is sick to his stomach" at the racial mixing that was going on at Azusa. Later his wife explained, "In Texas, you know, the colored people are not allowed to mix with the white people."[3] Parham was a full-fledged racist and an open supporter of the Ku Klux Klan. In time, he succeeded in drawing away almost three hundred whites from Azusa to start a rival group, but his ministry ended in disgrace because of his arrest in connection with a sex scandal.

William H. Durham, an influential Holiness leader from Chicago, moved to Los Angeles and at first seemed to join Seymour, but before long he publicly challenged some of Seymour's doctrinal beliefs and ultimately split off about six hundred of Seymour's followers—mostly white.

By the end of 1906 there were nine Pentecostal assemblies in Los Angeles. This would have been great, but some were not on good terms with others, and in the end Seymour's dedication to racial unity suffered as the groups, both there and elsewhere, became increasingly segregated and placed more and more emphasis on speaking in tongues and other "signs" rather than unity as proof of the baptism in the Holy Spirit.

On May 13, 1908, Seymour married Jennie Evans Moore, a dedicated member of his church. Clara Lum, mission secretary for the Azusa Street Mission, left Los Angeles and moved to Portland, Oregon—possibly out of jealousy, since she opposed the marriage—where she joined with minister Florence Crawford. However, without permission she took with her the national and foreign mailing lists for Seymour's newspaper. She then commenced publishing the paper from Portland as though it were still Seymour doing the writing and editing. Only later did she admit in print that she had taken over as editor. The Seymours went to Portland and tried, without success, to get Clara Lum to return the mailing lists. With only the Los Angeles area addresses, the influence of Seymour's paper quickly declined.

Nevertheless, the Pentecostal movement continued to expand until by 1914 it was represented in every American city of three thousand or more people and in every area of the world from Iceland to Tasmania, publishing literature in thirty languages.

Several major denominations grew out of the Azusa Street Revival. One example involves Bishop Charles H. Mason, who attended in 1907. He experienced the outpouring of the Holy Spirit and returned to his home in Jackson, Mississippi, to reorganize the Church of God in Christ. His ministry included a concern for all people, black and white. However, in 1914, because of heightened racial tension, a white segment split away from the main body and formed the Assemblies of God denomination. As years passed and the various Pentecostal denominations grew, William Seymour and his commitment to unity among Christians of every race was largely overlooked. The work at 312 Azusa Street continued in relative obscurity until Seymour died of heart failure on September 22, 1922. His wife carried on the declining ministry, but after her death in 1936, even the building was lost in 1938 because of unpaid taxes.

However, in 1994 and again in 1997, leaders of the Assemblies of God, the Church of God in Christ, and various other Pentecostal and charismatic groups met to pursue reconciliation and eliminate racism in their congregations. These efforts have involved formal expressions of repentance and apologies from white leaders and a celebration in which whites and blacks washed one another's feet.

Church historians are finally starting to realize the importance of Bishop William J. Seymour and his vision for Christian unity. As early as 1972, Sidney Ahlstrom, the noted church historian from

Yale University, made this remarkable claim: "Seymour exerted greater influence upon American Christianity than any other black leader."[4]

---

[1] William Seymour, *The Apostolic Faith,* June to September 1907, p. 2.

[2] Ibid.

[3] Parham, Mrs. Charles, *The Life of Charles W. Parham* (Birmingham, Alabama: Commercial Printing Co., 1930), p. 137.

[4] Ahlstrom, Sydney E., *A Religious History of the American People* (New Haven, Conn.: Yale University Press, 1971).

For Further Reading . . .

Bartleman, Frank, *Azusa Street* (Plainfield, New Jersey: Logos International, 1980).

Like as of Fire, reprints of all issues of *The Apostolic Faith* newspaper edited by William J. Seymour, 1906–08 (Washington, D.C.: Middle Atlantic Regional Press, 1994).

Nelson, Douglas J., *For Such a Time as This: The Story of Bishop William J. Seymour and the Azusa Street Revival* (Birmingham, England: University of Birmingham, 1981). Copies of this unpublished PhD. dissertation are available only in certain university libraries, but it is the most comprehensive review of Seymour available.

Story, Tim, and Leon Isaac Kennedy, *From Tragedy to Triumph: The William Seymour Story* (Whittier, Calif.: CTL Productions, 1992). Video.

Synan, Vinson, ed., *Aspects of Pentecostal-Charismatic Origins* (Plainfield, New Jersey: Logos International, 1975).

Synan, Vinson, *The Holiness-Pentecostal Movement in the United States* (Grand Rapids, Mich.: Wm. B. Eerdmans Publishing Co., 1977).